The Nutcracker Ballet Mystery

Nancy and George looked over the collection of props and boxes in the prop room. "Before we leave this afternoon, I have to make sure those tree ornaments aren't here," Nancy told her friend.

"Maybe we should move the pillar out of the way, so we can reach the boxes behind it," George said. "I'll push from behind. You stay in front and keep it from falling forward."

The girls were able to move the pillar about a foot before it began to topple. As she and George steadied the column, Nancy looked up. The ceiling was so dark, she couldn't see very well. But when she stepped back she saw something that startled her. Perched on the top of the pillar was a wooden nutcracker doll. It grinned down at her with a sinister smile.

"George, stop!" Nancy cried as the three-foot-tall doll began to teeter on the edge of the pillar.

But Nancy's warning came too late. The nutcracker doll toppled from the column—heading straight for George's head!

Nancy Drew
Mystery Stories

Available from MINSTREL Books

$$\boxed{110}$$

NANCY DREW®

THE NUTCRACKER BALLET MYSTERY

CAROLYN KEENE

A MINSTREL® BOOK

PUBLISHED BY POCKET BOOKS

New York London Toronto Sydney Tokyo Singapore

This book is a work of fiction. Names, characters, places, and incidents are either products of the author's imagination or are used fictitiously. Any resemblance to actual events or locales or persons, living or dead, is entirely coincidental.

A MINSTREL PAPERBACK *ORIGINAL*

A Minstrel Book published by
POCKET BOOKS, a division of Simon & Schuster Inc.
1230 Avenue of the Americas, New York, NY 10020

Copyright © 1992 by Simon & Schuster Inc.

Produced by Mega-Books of New York, Inc.

ISBN: 0-671-73056-8

First Minstrel Books printing December 1992

10   9   8   7   6   5

NANCY DREW, NANCY DREW MYSTERY STORIES, A MINSTREL BOOK and colophon are registered trademarks of Simon & Schuster Inc.

Cover art by Aleta Jenks

Printed in the U.S.A.

Contents

1

Ticket to Trouble

"I just love *The Nutcracker Ballet!*" George Fayne declared. Opening a copy of the River Heights morning newspaper, she showed her best friend, Nancy Drew, the ad for the ballet. It was being performed by Madame Dugrand's Dance Academy, a local ballet school.

"I'm glad we're getting a chance to see the performance this year," George added as she pulled off her lavender ski hat and shook out her short dark curls. "Remember when we danced in it?" she asked Nancy.

"I sure do," Nancy said, a smile on her face. "It must have been about eight years ago. Whenever I think of *The Nutcracker*, all I remember is Bess tripping over a mouse tail and knocking both of us into the Christmas tree."

"We didn't make very good soldiers, did we?"

1

With a chuckle, George folded the newspaper and put it back on the dashboard of Nancy's Mustang.

"Let's hope Madame Dugrand's latest students at the dance school are more dedicated." Nancy gave her shoulder-length blond hair a toss as she started the blue sports car. The two friends, who were both eighteen years old, were heading out of the state park, where they had just finished cross-country skiing.

"Bess couldn't wait to get away from dance class, remember?" Nancy went on. "All those arabesques and pliés were not her idea of fun."

"That's for sure," George agreed. "Which is why I can't believe my crazy cousin Bess is actually working at Madame Dugrand's school today."

Nancy gave George a puzzled look. "I thought she was shopping for Christmas presents."

"She's helping sew costumes," George said. "She met Madame Dugrand at the mall the other day. They started talking about *The Nutcracker*, and Madame said she was afraid the show wasn't going to be ready on time."

"Why?" Nancy raised her brows. "The dance school puts on *The Nutcracker* every year, so don't they already have the costumes and props?"

"I think Bess is helping to alter some of the costumes to fit the dancers," George explained. "Anyway, Madame told Bess that the rent for the school unexpectedly went way up, and the building needs a lot of repairs. I guess Madame is hoping this year's production will be super-sensational to help pay for everything. So she wants the show to be perfect. And you know what a soft touch Bess is. She immediately volunteered to help with the costumes."

"Mmmm," Nancy said thoughtfully. "Plus, it was her way of getting out of going cross-country skiing with us."

George laughed. "You're probably right. Bess can sew sitting down, so it won't seem like work to her. I also have a hunch Bess volunteered so she could hang out with Shana Edwards."

"Shana always was really nice," Nancy agreed as she passed a slower-moving car. "I guess we always knew she'd be the one from River Heights to make it as a ballerina in New York City. But The New York Ballet Company performs their own *Nutcracker*. Wouldn't you think Shana would rather dance in that one?"

"Bess said Shana came back because Madame Dugrand asked her to," George explained. "Madame hopes that having a famous alumna in the school's production will help make it a big success."

"I hope she's right," Nancy said. "I've always liked Madame Dugrand, and I know how important the ballet school is to her."

"Hey, why don't we stop off there right now?" George suggested. "We can surprise Bess, and take her to lunch with us."

"Good idea." Nancy flipped on the turn signal and made a right down Main Street. "I need to buy a ticket to the gala in Shana's honor, anyway."

George sighed. "I wish I could go to the gala, too. But the competitors' party for the cross-country ski race is that same night."

"Maybe Shana will be there today," Nancy said. After turning into the parking lot of the dance school, she pulled the Mustang into the first empty spot.

The school was located in a flat, rectangular building that had once been a small warehouse. Madame Dugrand had installed rows of tall windows into the brick walls and added skylights to the roof. Inside, she'd built two large dance studios, dressing rooms, an office for herself, and a large recital hall.

"The place looks just like it always did," George remarked as the girls headed up the snowy walk to the double front doors. Just then, she hit a patch of ice. "Whoa!" she cried as her feet slipped underneath her.

Nancy grabbed her friend's elbow, but it was too late. George fell to the sidewalk with a plop. "Are you okay?" Nancy asked. She couldn't help but grin at her friend's disgruntled expression.

"Yeah," George said. "I can't believe it. I skied all morning and never fell once."

Nancy helped her friend up. "I don't think it's your fault," she said. "The sidewalk should've had sand or salt on it. Remember how Madame was always so careful? She didn't want one of her precious ballerinas to hurt themselves."

"We'd better tell her, then," George said, slapping the snow off the back of her pants.

As they continued up the walk, Nancy saw that the ice hadn't been cleared from the steps, either. "This is pretty dangerous," she commented.

But George had already entered the building. When Nancy stepped into the hall beside her friend, she quickly noticed the chipping paint on the walls and the scuffed linoleum floor.

"Brings back old memories, huh?" George said.

Nancy nodded. "Bess was right, though. The place is a lot more run-down than I remember."

"Repairs are expensive," George said as the two of them started down the hall. "And Bess told me that, because of the rent increase, Madame's strapped for money. This year she's been teaching most of the classes herself, with help from some of the older students, who get a tuition break."

"That means less money coming in," Nancy pointed out. "Let's hope for Madame Dugrand's sake that bringing Shana back will draw a huge crowd for *The Nutcracker*."

"Speaking of ballerinas," George said, stopping in the front foyer and looking around the empty halls, "where is everyone?"

Nancy could hear the faint sound of piano music. "They must be in class."

"Bess is probably in the wardrobe room," George said.

"It was in the basement, right?" Nancy said. "Let's go look for her there."

The girls started down the dimly lit stairs. Cobwebs hung from the high ceiling.

"I don't think I'd like to come down here alone," George whispered. "It's kind of—"

"Who's there?" someone called in a shrill voice, cutting George off. An elderly woman with a cane hobbled into the dark, narrow hall below. Stopping at the foot of the stairs, she peered up at them through round granny glasses. Her wispy, snow-white hair looked like a halo around her forehead.

"I'm Nancy Drew," Nancy said politely. "And this is George Fayne. We're here to see—"

"Nancy! George!" Bess exclaimed, coming out of the wardrobe room and stopping beside the elderly woman. "What a nice surprise. How was the skiing?"

"Great," George said as she and Nancy made their way down the rest of the steps. "We stopped by to see if you wanted to have lunch with us."

Bess glanced over at the elderly woman, then said hesitantly, "I don't know if I should. I'm in the middle of putting lace on Clara's nightgown."

The white-haired woman smiled kindly. "Go eat, dear. You deserve a break."

"Oh, all right," Bess said. "But first, I want to show my friends your handiwork." After introducing Gertrude Wolaski to Nancy and George, Bess said, "Mrs. Wolaski is the most talented seamstress in the world."

6

"Now, Bess," Mrs. Wolaski said, shaking her head modestly. "Don't carry on."

"I'm not carrying on," Bess insisted. "You're a magician with a needle and thread."

"That's only because I spent thirty years of my life sewing for my husband's dry cleaning business," Mrs. Wolaski informed the girls.

Bess led the way down the short hall and into a medium-sized room. Long fluorescent lights shone down on several racks of costumes. Two sewing machines were set up on large tables littered with scissors, straight pins, and patterns. Spools of thread were stored on racks on the walls, next to bolts of many-colored fabrics.

Now that Nancy was standing next to the elderly woman, she could see how tiny she was. Mrs. Wolaski's rounded shoulders and hunched back made her look even smaller.

"How'd you get into the costume business?" Nancy asked, waving at the rows of gowns, mice suits, soldier uniforms, and ballet tutus.

Mrs. Wolaski laughed. "Well, I love the ballet. About a month ago I was at a recital here at the school and mentioned to Madame Dugrand that I used to sew. And as you know, Madame can be very persuasive. So I volunteered to help with the *Nutcracker* costumes. Not that an old lady like me has anything better to do." The wardrobe mistress smiled. "Now, if you'll excuse me, I must find Lawrence. He promised to pick up more pink tulle for me yesterday."

The girls said goodbye, then watched as Mrs.

Wolaski limped slowly back into the hall with the aid of her cane.

When the woman had gone, Bess grabbed Nancy's hand. "I want you both to see the Sugar Plum Fairy costume Mrs. Wolaski is making for Shana," she said excitedly. Riffling through a rack of costumes, Bess pulled out a dress with a bodice of shimmering silver satin and a skirt of wispy silver tulle. Clusters of pink beads decorated both the shoulder straps and the skirt.

"It's beautiful," Nancy said, touching the gossamer fabric.

"It looks expensive," George commented. "I thought Madame was trying to save money."

"Shana's costume had to be special, but we're just altering most of the others." Bess hung up the Sugar Plum costume, then pulled out a soldier uniform. "Does this remind you of anything?" she asked, a twinkle in her blue eyes. "Like opening night of *The Nutcracker* when I stole the show?"

"Is that what you did?" Nancy teased as she and George burst out laughing. "I thought you fell on George and me, and we all knocked the big Christmas tree over."

"Well, maybe it was more like that." Bess giggled, then frowned slightly. "Let's hope this year's *Nutcracker* is more successful. Nothing else seems to be going right for Madame Dugrand."

Nancy raised her brows. "You mean like the rent increase?"

"It's worse than just that," Bess said. "A lot of

little things have been happening around here, and they're beginning to add up."

"Like what?" George asked.

Bess's voice dropped to a whisper. "Well, two girls had toe shoes stolen from their lockers. And there's been a lot of bickering among the kids and parents, too, about who got what part."

"There was always grumbling," Nancy reminded her. "I mean, even though we weren't very good dancers, we still thought we should've had the lead roles." Bess slid the soldier uniform back with the others. "Yeah, but this seems different. Madame's so nervous it's affecting everyone."

"How's Shana taking all of this?" George asked. "She did come all the way from New York for the production."

"I don't know if Shana has any idea of what's going on," Bess said, taking her coat from the back of a chair. "But I do know she wants to see you both."

"Great," George said.

"Let me buy a ticket to the gala, then we can find Shana and say hello," Nancy suggested.

"Good idea," Bess said.

The girls headed upstairs, where the hallway was no longer empty. This time, several older boys and girls dressed in sweats and leotards were limbering up before the next class.

When Nancy, George, and Bess reached Madame Dugrand's office, the door was open. Looking over Bess's shoulder, Nancy noticed that the

9

small area was filled with file folders and papers. Madame Dugrand, a slim, attractive woman in her early fifties, was sitting in a swivel chair behind an old-fashioned rolltop desk. The desk was cluttered with papers and envelopes, and to the right of it was a computer on a stand.

Bess knocked on the door frame, and Madame looked up from an open ledger. When she saw who it was, she smiled brightly. Nancy thought that despite her gray hair, Madame hadn't aged since they'd been students eight years ago.

"Bess!" the directress exclaimed, standing up. "How do the costumes look?"

"Great. The Sugar Plum Fairy costume is a work of art." Bess stepped into the office, then motioned to Nancy and George. "I brought two former students to see you. And one of them wants to buy a gala ticket."

Madame's smile widened. "Nancy Drew and George Fayne! What a pleasant surprise!"

"Nancy's the one who needs a ticket," George explained. "I wish I could go to the gala, too," she added quickly, "but I have a party that night after a cross-country race."

"You always were athletic," Madame Dugrand told her. "And, Nancy, what are you up to these days?"

"She's only the best teen detective in the world," Bess cut in.

Nancy laughed. "Not exactly 'the best.'"

"Well, I'm glad you'll be able to come to the gala," Madame said as she opened her desk

10

drawer and hunted for the tickets. "As I recall, you three used to know Shana—"

Suddenly, a high-pitched alarm went off.

Bess jumped nervously. "What's that?"

In a flash, Madame Dugrand rushed past the girls and into the hall. "The fire alarm," she called over her shoulder.

Following Madame Dugrand into the hallway, Nancy asked, "Was there a fire drill scheduled for today?"

"No!" Madame exclaimed, breaking into a jog. "This must be a real fire!"

2

Old Times, New Crimes

"We have to get the students out of the building right away!" Madame Dugrand's voice was frantic.

Nancy knew they had to hurry. A faint whiff of smoke was already drifting down the hall. Bess and George were right behind her. "Bess!" Nancy called. "Phone the fire department. Then run down to the basement and make sure Mrs. Wolaski heard the fire alarm."

With a nod, Bess picked up the office phone. "I'll check to see that the locker room is cleared," George said, heading through a swinging door.

Nancy and Madame Dugrand raced down the hall and into the first studio.

An older girl was standing in the center of the room, a panic-stricken expression on her face.

Several kids were dashing back and forth, squealing loudly.

Madame Dugrand clapped her hands several times. "Quiet!" she commanded. "Line up behind Miss Sarah."

Realizing Madame Dugrand had the situation in hand, Nancy rushed to the next room. A tall, striking red-haired woman was waving a dozen girls in leotards toward the doorway. Nancy realized the redhead was Shana Edwards.

"Class! Get in line!" Shana ordered in a firm voice.

Nancy grabbed two young boys as they attempted to dash by her and pushed them into the line behind Shana. "Quickly, you must leave the building!" Nancy said as she helped herd the group into the hall.

Bess dashed up beside her. "The basement's empty," she gasped. "Mrs. Wolaski must already be outside."

A girl about nine years old stopped and tugged on Nancy's sleeve. "What about our coats?" she asked. Her hair was the same shade of red as Shana's. "Can't we run into the dressing room for them?"

Bess shook her head. "No, Michelle. We must do what we did during our drill earlier this week. Now, hurry and follow your sister." She gave the girl a gentle push toward the outside door.

"That's Shana's little sister, Michelle," Bess whispered to Nancy as they hurried to check the

13

recital hall. "She's Clara in *The Nutcracker* this year."

Bess helped Nancy open the double doors into the recital hall. The two of them peered inside. The long rows of chairs and dark stage looked empty. Nancy sniffed the air.

"I smell smoke," she said.

"Then let's get out of here." Swinging around, Bess started toward the hall. For a second, Nancy hesitated. If she could locate the fire and put it out, it might prevent damage to the building.

Bess gave Nancy's arm an urgent tug. "I know what you're thinking, Nancy Drew, and don't you dare. You leave the fire to the fire fighters."

"You're right." Quickly, Nancy and Bess shut the doors and jogged down the now empty hall. They met George at the outside doors. She was ushering the last of the children down the slippery steps and into the parking lot.

"Is everybody out?" Madame Dugrand asked from the sidewalk. She was standing in the middle of a shivering group of youngsters. The sky was dark with clouds, and a light snow was beginning to fall.

"Yes," Nancy called back. The blast of a siren made her look out into the street. A huge River Heights fire truck careened into the parking lot.

Racing down the icy sidewalk, Nancy met the first fireman off the truck.

"We smelled smoke in the recital hall." She pointed toward the left side of the building.

14

Waving to the others, the fireman headed in that direction.

As Nancy walked back to George and Bess, she scanned the small crowd huddled in front of the dance school. Shana Edwards was leading two kids toward a waiting car. Mrs. Wolaski was hobbling down the walk, holding on to the arm of a blond-haired young man about twenty years old. Several parents had driven up in front of the school. Madame Dugrand was separating their children from the group gathered on the sidewalk.

"Madame Dugrand," Nancy called as she strode across the snow-covered grass, "maybe we should get the kids into our cars. It'll be warmer."

"That's a good idea, Nancy. Thank you for your help."

Just then a woman wearing a purple warm-up suit pushed past Nancy. A frightened-looking little girl in a leotard and tights clung to her hand.

"This fire is the last straw, Alicia!" the woman declared to Madame Dugrand. "I quit. You'll have to get someone else to organize the props. And you'll have to replace Tiffany, too. I'm pulling her out of *The Nutcracker*—and the school."

With that, the woman spun around, dragging the unhappy little girl after her.

Madame Dugrand's face flushed brightly. But

15

she quickly leaned down to a young boy who was clinging to her leg. "Here's something to keep you warm, Patrick," she said as she took off her sweater and wrapped it around his shoulders.

When she straightened, she signaled to the blond-haired young man with a wave of her hand. "Lawrence! Unlock the van. We'll put as many students in it as we can."

For the next few minutes, Nancy helped Lawrence, George, Bess, and Madame get the children settled in the van and in her Mustang. Several more parents picked up their kids, so there was room enough for everyone. Soon only Nancy and Madame Dugrand were left outside in the snow. Fire fighters were streaming in and out of the building, but Nancy hadn't seen any fire or smelled any more smoke.

"What do you think caused the fire?" Nancy asked.

Shaking her head, Madame wrapped her arms tighter across her chest. She was looking worriedly toward the school. Her shoulders were hunched, and a light sprinkling of snow covered her gray hair. Just then, the fire chief strode down the steps. Nancy followed Madame Dugrand as she walked up the sidewalk to meet him.

"It appears that someone accidentally started a fire," the chief said in a stern voice. "Part of your backstage curtain was burning." He held up a cigarette enclosed in a plastic bag. "I suspect it was caused by this."

16

Madame gasped. "I do *not* allow smoking in the building," she said indignantly.

The fire chief shrugged. "Someone broke the rules." He stuck the bag under his coat, then pulled a pad and a pen out of his back pocket.

"Actually," the chief continued, "whoever set the fire probably did you a favor, Ms. Dugrand. Your building has several fire violations. Frayed wires, paint-soaked rags, and an exit blocked with chairs. It's no wonder the whole place didn't go up in flames. This," he said, ripping the top sheet from the pad and handing it to Madame Dugrand, "is a citation. All the items on this list need to be corrected by next Friday or the fire department will close you down."

Madame Dugrand's face turned ashen as her blue eyes traveled down the list. "Next Friday is our opening night," she said, looking up.

The chief shrugged again. "That's your problem. Fires are mine, and I don't want one here. You can all go on in now," he added brusquely. Then he turned to his crew and yelled, "Let's pack it up, guys!"

Madame Dugrand didn't move. Her eyes were frozen on the citation in her hand.

"We'd better get the kids back into the school," Nancy said gently.

With a deep sigh, Madame nodded. Twenty minutes later, the students who hadn't been picked up by their parents were back in class.

"I'm going to take a look at the burned curtain," Nancy told Bess and George.

17

"But the fire chief already checked everything, and I'm *starved*," Bess protested, but Nancy was already starting down the hall.

"Hey!" a voice called. Nancy turned to see Shana Edwards coming out of the locker room. She was tall and slender, wearing a fuchsia leotard and pink tights. Her red hair was pulled back and tucked into a chignon, accenting her long neck and straight posture.

"Nancy Drew!" Shana exclaimed, her emerald eyes sparkling. "I was hoping I'd see you." Just then she spotted George. The girls gave each other warm hugs.

"And we were hoping to see the famous Shana Edwards," George said, holding her old friend at arm's length.

"Too famous to have lunch with some dance school dropouts?" Bess joked.

"Never," Shana replied. "I've got to work with Dewdrop and her flowers first, though. They've been having a little trouble with their scene. Would you guys like to watch? If you can stick around until it's over, we can talk then. I'd love to know what everyone in River Heights has been up to. You know, all the gossip."

Bess rolled her eyes. "Oh, it's *sooo* exciting around here."

The girls burst out laughing.

"And we'd love to hear all about New York," George added.

"Great." Shana squeezed Nancy's hand. "And

thanks, guys, for all the help during the fire alarm. Whew! What a madhouse."

"No problem," Nancy replied. "Listen, I've got to pick up my ticket for the gala, then I'll meet you guys in—"

"Studio A," Shana filled in. Then, linking her arms with Bess's and George's, she hurried them down the hall.

Nancy continued toward the stage area. She knew the fire chief had probably been thorough, but maybe he hadn't looked beyond the cigarette. Even Nancy wasn't sure what she should be looking for. Had the fire been deliberately set? Bess had said earlier that strange things were going on at the school. Unfortunately, except for a few scenery panels that were being painted, the stage was empty. The firemen had removed the torn curtain, and Nancy couldn't find anything that looked suspicious.

When she got back to Madame Dugrand's office, Nancy found the ballet directress sitting at her desk, a worried frown creasing her brow.

After Nancy bought a ticket to the gala, she said, "I'm really sorry about the fire."

Madame Dugrand forced a thin smile. "Oh, the fire is just one more problem to add to a long list. Mrs. Patterson, the mother who quit and took her daughter with her, was in charge of the props for the show." Madame threw up her hands. "I just don't have time to organize the props. This year's *Nutcracker* is turning into a disaster."

"Maybe I can help," Nancy offered.

Madame Dugrand's blue eyes brightened. "Do you mean it? Oh, that would be wonderful, Nancy!" she exclaimed.

"I'll start tomorrow," Nancy promised.

"I can't thank you enough," declared the directress, getting to her feet. "Now, I must find Lawrence."

"Who's Lawrence?" Nancy asked.

"Lawrence Steele dances here at the school. He'll be the Cavalier dancing opposite the Sugar Plum Fairy. He also teaches classes and helps me with the maintenance of the building. He needs to get right to work on correcting those fire code violations."

Nancy frowned. "That reminds me. Do you know which fire alarm was set off?" she asked, following Madame Dugrand into the hallway.

The directress nodded. "The smoke detector over the stage went off automatically."

That didn't sound suspicious, Nancy thought. Maybe she should quit hunting for a mystery.

When Nancy reached studio A, Shana was standing next to a small, pinch-faced man in his early twenties. He was sitting at a big, black upright piano, frowning at the sheet of music propped in front of him. In the middle of the bare wooden floor, nine girls about sixteen years old were limbering up.

"See that girl over there?" Bess said when Nancy rejoined her and George. The cousins were sitting on a bench in front of a mirrored wall. Skylights brightened the windowless room.

"Which one?" Nancy asked as she sat down.

"The one with the purple tights." Bess pointed toward a pretty girl with shiny chestnut hair and green eyes. "That's Darci Edwards."

"That's right. There are three Edwards sisters," George remarked. "They all look alike."

Bess nodded. "And all three of them are talented. Darci's dancing Dewdrop in the Dance of the Flowers."

"And who's that?" Nancy asked, nodding toward the piano player. "I didn't see him outside."

"That's Roger Lutz, the accompanist," Bess replied. "He only works here part-time. He's still in music school, I think. He's playing piano for Madame to get more experience. Maybe he arrived after the fire alarm."

"He looks like a mouse," George said.

"He's quiet like one, too," Bess added. "At least, he never talks to anyone. Madame Dugrand likes him, though. She'd been using tapes in her classes, but real music is so much better. Then Roger showed up about a month ago, saying he needed the experience. Plus, he knew Madame had contacts in New York for when he graduated from music school."

Just then Shana looked their way. Nancy waved. Shana smiled and waved back, then walked over.

21

"You're just in time. The girls and I are going to warm up at the barre." She pointed to the long wooden pole attached to the far wall. "Then we'll put on our toe shoes and do some floor work."

"It sounds exciting!" Bess gushed.

"Believe me, it's work." Shana chuckled as she gracefully walked to the center of the room. When she clapped her hands, each dancer found a place at the barre.

Shana went to the shorter demonstration barre at the side of the room. She nodded at Roger, and he began playing a slow, dramatic piece.

Placing her hand lightly on the barre, Shana slowly extended her right leg in front of her.

"Shana makes everything look so easy," Nancy whispered, leaning closer to Bess.

Her friend giggled. "Only *we* know how hard it is. I never could get my leg up on that stupid— Oh, no!" Bess suddenly gasped.

Nancy swung her head around to look at Shana. The barre had pulled clean away from the wall, crashing down on Shana's support leg. With a cry of pain, the dancer toppled backward, landing awkwardly on the hard, wooden floor.

3

Partners in Spite

Nancy, Bess, and George raced to the fallen dancer's side. Roger Lutz, the accompanist, reached Shana first.

"Take the other end of the pole," he told the girls in a low voice. Together, the four of them lifted the barre off Shana's ankle.

"Are you all right?" Nancy asked, helping Shana sit up.

"I—I think so," Shana said uncertainly. She probed her ankle with her fingers. "Just bruised," she added, taking a shaky breath.

Meanwhile, Shana's students had formed a half-circle around her.

"Can you stand up?" Bess asked.

"I'll try," Shana said. She extended a hand toward Nancy. Roger supported her other elbow, and together they helped Shana to her feet. As

23

soon as she was standing, all of her students applauded . . . all except Shana's sister, Darci, Nancy noticed. Darci's arms remained folded across her chest. Then she turned abruptly and went back to the other barre.

Nancy was puzzled. She would have thought Shana's sister would be the most concerned.

"Careful, Shana," one of the other students said. "You don't want to pull a tightened muscle."

"You're right, April," Shana agreed. She was still holding on to Nancy's arm, her weight off her bruised leg. "I think I'd better reschedule this class for later. You girls can go. I'll post the new time after I talk to Madame Dugrand."

"What about me?" Roger said in a sulky voice. "I may not be available later."

Nancy looked up at him. He had thin, brown hair, and a sparse mustache dusted his upper lip. George was right, Nancy thought. He really did look like a mouse.

"I understand," Shana said, nodding. "I'll just have to use a tape, if that's the case."

"Fine," Roger grunted. Not bothering to hide his annoyance, he returned to the piano and quickly gathered up his music. The other students were already collecting the dance bags, leg warmers, towels, and shawls that they'd left scattered about the room.

"What's his problem?" George asked Shana when Roger and the students had left. She and Nancy were helping Shana over to the bench.

"The same problem everyone else around here has," Shana replied, limping awkwardly.

"Madame calls it preperformance jitters," Bess explained as Shana sat down.

Shana shook her head. "I'm afraid it's more than that, Bess. I've been in quite a few shows both here and in New York. Things can get pretty tense before a performance all right, but I've never experienced anything like this."

"I guess the fire didn't help," George said. "And the barre falling like that was kind of strange. But when things get run down, as they have in this place, accidents do happen."

"That might explain the falling ballet barre, George," Nancy said, "but it doesn't explain the stealing Bess mentioned."

"Stealing?" Shana's brows raised. "I hadn't heard about that."

"Two days ago, Tiffany Patterson's toe shoes disappeared, then Maria Ramirez's tutu," Bess explained.

"So that's why Mrs. Patterson was so mad," Nancy said thoughtfully. "She told Madame Dugrand that the fire was the last straw. Then she quit as the prop manager, and she also withdrew Tiffany from the school."

"Oh, no!" Bess exclaimed. "That's the third student this week." She sighed. "Mrs. Wolaski said the parents didn't think the level of professionalism was high enough."

"With Mrs. Patterson gone, who'll be in charge of props?" Shana asked.

Nancy grinned. "Me. And I'm sure my good friend George will help when she's not training for her race." Nancy threw an arm around George's shoulders, and all three girls looked at George expectantly.

"Okay, okay," George said with a laugh. "You guys would probably toss me into a snowdrift if I said no."

"Well, at least that problem's solved." Shana sighed. "I mean, I sure want to help Madame. I owe her so much. But I don't want to get injured doing it." She glanced back at the fallen barre.

"I don't blame you." Nancy walked over to the wooden pole. Kneeling down, she examined the ends of the barre, then looked up at the wall from which it had fallen.

"I don't think the barre came away from the wall by accident," Nancy said with a frown. Standing up, she turned to face the others. "Someone deliberately loosened it."

"How can you tell?" Shana asked.

"There should have been four screws on each of the brackets that hold the barre to the wall." Nancy recrossed the room and showed the girls the screws she'd found. "All together there should be eight screws, but I only found these two."

"Maybe the others rolled away or something," Bess suggested.

Nancy shook her head. "One or two screws might roll away. But not six. Someone removed

26

most of them, knowing that the remaining ones couldn't support a dancer's weight."

"Are you saying someone tried to hurt me on purpose?" Shana asked, her eyes wide with disbelief.

Nancy shook her head. "I don't know. Were you the only teacher using studio A today?"

Shana thought for a moment, then nodded slowly. "I think so."

"Maybe the fire and the falling barre are related," George said. "Someone set the fire, and when the place was empty, they sneaked in and unscrewed the screws."

"But who would do that?" Bess asked. "And why?"

"It doesn't make sense," Shana added, rubbing her ankle. "Why would someone want to hurt me?"

"I don't know," Nancy admitted. "But I intend to find out."

Shana looked relieved. "Thanks, Nancy. I'm sure you can do it. Even in New York, I remember reading about one of the cases you solved."

"Just remember, though, that my being on this case is strictly unofficial," Nancy cautioned everyone. "Madame Dugrand has enough on her mind—I don't want her thinking she has a case of serious crime on her hands, too. And there might not be anything going on here after all."

Slowly, Shana got to her feet. "Well, I'd better put some ice on this. I'm afraid I'm going to have to pass on lunch."

"Do you want some help?" Bess asked. But Shana shook her head as she walked slowly to the piano to get her shawl and leg warmers.

"If you see or hear anything suspicious," Nancy called, "let me know, okay?"

"I will," Shana promised as George opened the door for her. Shana said goodbye, then hobbled down the hall and into the locker room.

"Her leg looks really sore," Bess said in a concerned voice. "I hope she's okay."

"And I hope this doesn't sound callous," George said, "but if I don't eat soon, *I* may not be okay."

Bess grinned. "Now you're talking, George! Let's go to Yogurt Heaven, just like old times."

A short time later, Nancy was parking her car in front of Yogurt Heaven, a longtime favorite hangout for students at the dance academy.

"I'm a little surprised this place is still here," George said, climbing out of Nancy's blue Mustang.

"It hasn't changed too much, either," Bess assured George. "They still serve the same fabulous low-cal yogurt that they did when we were students at Madame Dugrand's."

Once inside the restaurant, the girls found the booth they'd thought of as theirs when they were ten. Nancy and George slid in one side and Bess sat across from them. The waitress brought menus and water, then left.

"I'm going to have a turkey club sandwich,

then the pineapple delight with extra coconut," Bess declared eagerly.

"I'm too hungry to decide so quickly. What are you going to have, Nancy?" George asked.

"Shhh!" Nancy told her friends suddenly. She nodded toward the front door of the restaurant. "Isn't that Lawrence from the dance school?"

Peering over her shoulder, Bess nodded. "And Shana's sister, Darci."

"So what's the big deal about that?" George asked in a low voice.

"Nothing, I guess," Nancy replied. "But did you guys see how funny Darci acted after Shana fell? It looked as if she couldn't have cared less."

"Yeah, I noticed," George said. "Are Darci and Lawrence going together?" she asked Bess.

"I don't know," Bess replied. "But Darci did have her heart set on dancing with Lawrence in *The Nutcracker*. She wanted to be the Sugar Plum Fairy, but then Madame asked Shana to come back to dance the part."

"So Lawrence is partnering Shana now instead of Darci," Nancy said thoughtfully. "No wonder she gave her sister such a dirty look."

"I can see why Darci might be upset about the change," George said. "But I'd think Lawrence would be thrilled to have such a great dancer for his partner."

Bess leaned closer. "Oh, Lawrence has a

29

grudge against Shana, too. Mrs. Wolaski told me he was supposed to choreograph all the big dance scenes. But when Shana came back, Madame split the scenes between Shana and him. He was *not* happy."

Nancy looked back at the couple. Darci was standing awfully close to Lawrence, and his arm was casually around her shoulders. He had blond curly hair and a great dancer's build.

"I'd say Lawrence was at least a couple of years older than Darci," Bess commented.

George and Nancy agreed. Just then, the two dancers started down the aisle toward them. Quickly, Nancy stuck the menu in front of her face. George and Bess did the same.

After picking up two sundaes at the counter, Lawrence and Darci took the booth directly behind the girls. They were close enough for Nancy to hear their conversation.

"You should have seen it, Lawrence," Darci said delightedly. "One minute Miss High and Mighty Shana was up there showing off for everyone, and the next moment she was flat on the floor. It was a total wipeout!"

Lawrence laughed. "That's just what Shana needs to bring her back down to earth. I wish I'd been there to see it."

"Maybe another little accident might convince Shana to go back to New York where she belongs," Darci suggested.

"I don't know," Lawrence said slowly. He paused, as if he might say something more.

Holding her breath, Nancy leaned closer toward their booth. She didn't want to miss a word.

"I have a feeling it will probably take more than just a *little* accident to get rid of that sister of yours," Lawrence continued. "And knowing you, Darci, you're just the person to think of one!"

4

Accidents Will Happen

Bess's eyebrows shot up. "That sounds like a threat," she whispered excitedly.

Nancy nodded and put her finger to her lips. It definitely seemed as if Darci Edwards could have played a part in her sister's accident. But why? Was she that angry because Shana had gotten the role of the Sugar Plum Fairy?

Nancy remembered that Mr. and Mrs. Edwards had been very ambitious for their three daughters. Maybe they'd pushed too hard, and the girls had ended up competing with one another.

Nancy's thoughts were interrupted when the waitress asked, "What will you ladies have?"

While Bess and George ordered, Nancy listened to Lawrence and Darci discuss Darci's part in *The Nutcracker*. Darci didn't sound happy about being Dewdrop at all.

Once Darci and Lawrence were gone and Nancy had ordered her food, she said, "I guess Darcy is pretty angry at her sister."

"Angry!" Bess exclaimed. "Isn't that sort of an understatement? Darci and Lawrence both want to get rid of Shana."

"Neither of them actually admitted removing the screws from the demonstration barre," George pointed out.

Nancy nodded. "George is right. The only thing we know for sure is that Darci and Lawrence both have reasons why they're angry at Shana," she said. "That's not exactly a crime. But . . ." Pausing, she tapped her spoon on the table in thought.

"But what?" George prompted.

Nancy pointed the spoon at George. "But if I were Darci and Lawrence, I'd be pretty mad at Madame Dugrand, too. After all, she's the one who asked Shana to come back."

"Mad enough that they'd try to ruin the school?" George asked. "That seems kind of drastic."

Bess shook her head. "We'd better warn Shana about those two."

"Not yet," Nancy cautioned. "We have to be careful. After all, Darci is Shana's sister."

"Still, I think we should keep our eyes on Darci and Lawrence," Bess said emphatically.

"I agree," Nancy said. "And now that George and I are in charge of props, tomorrow we'll be at the dance academy to do just that."

* * *

It was snowing Friday morning when Nancy parked her Mustang in front of the dance school.

"It looks as though George is going to have great snow for skiing this morning," Nancy said to Bess, tossing her keys into her shoulder bag as they got out of the car. George was meeting them at the dance school just before lunch.

With a shiver, Bess brushed away the snow-flakes that had landed on her nose. "George can have her skiing. Me, I'd rather be in a nice warm room."

Nancy laughed as the two of them carefully made their way up the still-icy walk. When they entered the dance school, Bess glanced at her watch. "It's nine o'clock now. When shall we break for lunch?"

"Come to the prop room around noon," Nancy suggested. "George should be here by then, and the three of us can eat together."

"I'll ask Mrs. Wolaski to join us, too," Bess said, starting downstairs. "I think she's kind of lonely since her husband died last year."

"Okay. See you then." Waving goodbye, Nancy headed down the main hall. The prop room was on the left-hand side, directly across from studio A.

Flicking on the lights, Nancy glanced around the large room. Boxes of every size and description littered the concrete floor. Some of them were stacked to the metal support beams that crisscrossed the ceiling. The unfinished room, with its brick walls and no windows, still looked

34

like an old warehouse. The place was cold, dusty, and damp.

Shivering, Nancy wrapped her coat tighter around her. She had no idea where to begin, and from the looks of things, Mrs. Patterson hadn't either. In addition to the boxes, the room was filled with larger props: everything from pieces of furniture to pink flamingos and even a bicycle. Nancy had almost decided to ask Madame Dugrand for help when she spotted what looked like a list taped to the wall.

Nancy wove her way around several painted panels that had fallen to the floor and checked the list. Nutcracker Props was printed in bold letters across the top of the first page. Many of the things on the list had been checked off.

"I hope that means they're accounted for," Nancy muttered to herself. Reading carefully through the entire list, she began to verify the checked items. Behind a stack of wood, she found the toy cannon that the soldiers would fire at the mice during their battle scene. And in the corner was the sled little Clara and her prince would ride to reach the Land of Sweets. Next on the list, Mrs. Patterson had checked off the Christmas tree ornaments.

Nancy looked at one stack of boxes. The ornaments could be in any of these, she thought. She carefully opened the boxes one by one, finding all kinds of props: tambourines, dolls, wrapped Christmas presents, as well as cans of paint and brushes. But she couldn't find any ornaments.

Nancy knew they were important. Without them, the Christmas tree in the party scene would look very bare.

Nancy let out a frustrated sigh. Great, she thought. First day on the job and I'm already missing something. Then she spied the back door that led to the recital hall stage. Maybe Mrs. Patterson had put the ornaments on stage already.

As she walked across the room, Nancy wiped her dirty hands on her jeans, then opened the door. Three steps led to the left side of offstage. The area was dark and quiet and smelled like stale smoke. For a second, Nancy hesitated. What if there *was* a saboteur, and he or she was lurking around ready to set another fire?

No, that was silly, she chided herself. Besides, if he or she was there, Nancy was ready to face the person.

Cautiously, she walked out onto the stage, hunting for the box. The big wooden Christmas tree was in the center of the stage, but there were no ornaments hanging on it. Then Nancy checked backstage, behind the heavy curtain. As she swept the curtain aside with her hand, she noticed something white on the floor beneath it.

She stooped to pick the object up. It was a white lace handkerchief with the initials *G. T.* embroidered on the edge.

G. T. Who involved in the dance school had those initials? Nancy wondered. With a shrug, she stuck the handkerchief in her back pocket and went back down the three steps into the prop room.

Making a quick decision, Nancy left the dark room and went into the main hall. She hated to disturb Madame Dugrand with one more problem, but she needed to find out where the ornaments were. If there weren't any, Nancy was going to have to come up with some before dress rehearsal the following Thursday. That was less than a week away.

"Excuse me," Nancy said, sticking her head into Madame Dugrand's office. The directress looked up from her paperwork. Through the window beside the desk, Nancy could see that the snow was falling faster.

"Nancy!" Madame Dugrand exclaimed. "How is everything going, dear?"

"I'm afraid I can't find the box of ornaments for the Christmas tree," Nancy replied. "They've been checked off the list, but they're not in the prop room or on the stage."

"What?" Madame sprang to her feet. "Oh, I hope they aren't lost! We're using Rebecca Farnsworth's ornaments this year, and they're priceless antiques."

"Maybe I overlooked them," Nancy said quickly. She hadn't realized how upset Madame would be. "Or maybe they were just checked off by mistake and haven't been delivered yet."

"Maybe." Walking around her desk, Madame began to pace up and down in front of Nancy. "But whatever happened, you *must* find them.

Those props are very important. See those pictures?" Madame added, pointing to the wall beside her desk.

Nancy nodded as she looked at the display of gold-framed photos.

"These particular pictures," Madame Dugrand said, gesturing toward a cluster of five photos, "are publicity shots from my former ballet company's *Nutcracker*."

Nancy moved closer for a better look. In one picture Clara was holding the Nutcracker doll, and in another the Candy Canes posed in the Land of Sweets. "It looks lovely," Nancy said.

"Thanks to the wonderful costumes and props we had," Madame said. "That's why I've collected them both so carefully over the years. Every season I try to add something new, a small treat for my faithful patrons. This year, the Farnsworth ornaments were to be that treat. That's why it's so important that we find them."

Nancy was about to swear she'd track down the ornaments no matter what when the phone rang. Madame Dugrand stretched gracefully across her desk to answer it.

After a moment of listening, Madame Dugrand slammed down the phone. "What will be next?" she exclaimed, throwing up her hands. "That was the printer. Someone canceled our Nutcracker programs earlier this week! Now the shop can't promise them on time!"

"That's awful!" Nancy tried to console the directress. "Look, please don't worry about the ornaments, Madame. I'll take care of them. And somehow we'll make sure this show is a success."

Explaining that she'd suddenly gotten an idea where the ornaments might be, Nancy hurried back to the prop room and retrieved her purse.

Fifteen minutes later, she drove up the circular drive in front of Rebecca Farnsworth's estate. The wealthy widow was involved in numerous charities in and around River Heights and was an outspoken patron of the arts as well.

Nancy rang the bell. Surprisingly, Mrs. Farnsworth herself came to the door.

"Hello, Mrs. Farnsworth," Nancy said. "I'm Nancy Drew."

The silver-haired woman smiled. "Why, yes. You're Carson Drew's daughter. Come in, my dear."

As she shut the heavy door, Mrs. Farnsworth inquired, "How is your father, Nancy?"

"He's fine, thank you," Nancy said politely. She wiped her snowy shoes on the mat and followed Mrs. Farnsworth into a huge, marble-tiled foyer.

Then Nancy decided to get right down to business. "I'm helping organize the props for *The Nutcracker Ballet,* and I came to pick up the ornaments you offered to lend the school."

Mrs. Farnsworth's eyebrows knitted together. "My chauffeur delivered those ornaments last Tuesday," she said, frowning. "He told me he handed them right to Marjorie Patterson."

"Oh, good," Nancy said with a big smile. "I'm

sure Mrs. Patterson put them in a safe place," she added quickly, not wanting Mrs. Farnsworth to know that the ornaments had disappeared.

Mrs. Farnsworth nodded. "I hope so. If anything should happen to those ornaments, I don't know what—"

"Oh, I'm sure they're very safe," Nancy fibbed, walking back toward the front door. "I'm terribly sorry I bothered you. And thanks again." She let herself out before Mrs. Farnsworth could say anything more.

Nancy pulled into the dance academy lot just as George drove up.

"Am I ever glad to see you," Nancy said.

"What's up?" George asked. "You look worried."

As the girls walked to the entrance, Nancy filled George in on the missing ornaments. "And all this means if Mrs. Patterson doesn't have them, we're in big trouble," Nancy concluded.

Using the pay phone in the hall, Nancy called the Patterson's house. Mrs. Patterson's answer made Nancy's heart sink.

"She said they're in the box inside the sled," Nancy told George when she'd hung up. "But there *isn't* any box in the sled."

George took off her coat and started down the hall. "Maybe you just overlooked it," she called over her shoulder.

An hour later, there were still no ornaments in sight.

"This is just great," Nancy said with a sigh as she sat back on her heels. George was kneeling beside her. The two of them were surrounded by open boxes full of props. "I have a hunch that whoever canceled the programs took the ornaments, too," Nancy said.

George shook her head. "Probably the same person who set off the fire alarm and loosened the demonstration barre in studio A."

"It does seem as if all these disasters are happening too close together not to be related," Nancy said.

"You still think it could be Lawrence and Darci?"

Nancy sighed again. "I wish I knew."

Just then, the girls heard tinkly *Nutcracker* music floating through the prop room's open door.

"Maybe we should take a break," George said.

With a nod, Nancy stood up. "You read my mind." When they reached studio A, Nancy slowly opened the door.

Lawrence and Shana were alone in the studio. A tape recorder on the piano was playing music from the Dance of the Sugar Plum Fairy.

As Nancy watched the two dancers, she almost forgot the harsh words she'd overheard Lawrence utter about Shana at Yogurt Heaven. The two dancers were rehearsing the romantic pas de deux from *The Nutcracker*.

Shana was supported against Lawrence's arm.

Dipping back, she arched her arms gracefully over her head. Then Lawrence spun Shana around, and with both hands on her waist, began to lift her high into the air. But the romantic mood disappeared when Lawrence suddenly lost his balance. Shana sailed backward over his head, a look of horror on her face!

5

Dangerous Playthings

Shana screamed as she flew over Lawrence's head toward the wooden floor.

"Oh, no!" George gasped, rushing with Nancy into the studio.

At the last second, Lawrence lurched forward and pulled Shana down to his shoulders. Her weight threw him sideways and he staggered. Then, finally getting his balance, he lowered her in front of him, setting her awkwardly on her feet.

"Are you all right?" he said. Lawrence's face was flushed, and his eyes were full of concern.

Angrily, Shana pulled away from him. "You klutz! I could have broken my neck!"

Nancy and George stopped short. Nancy was close enough to see Lawrence's expression of concern turn into one of startled annoyance.

"If that's all the thanks I get for saving you, maybe I should have dropped you," Lawrence retorted.

"Saving me! That's a laugh," Shana declared. "Nancy and George are witnesses to the fact that you deliberately dropped me. Right?" Hands on her hips, Shana turned toward the two girls.

"Witness to what?" Lawrence laughed sarcastically before Nancy or George could answer. "To your own clumsiness? Who are these two friends of yours, anyway? And why are they hanging around the school like they belong here?"

"Leave them out of this," Shana snapped. Taking a step toward Lawrence, she poked him in the chest with her index finger. "You're just trying to avoid the fact that your hands weren't in the right place on my waist."

"No way." Lawrence moved closer, towering over Shana. "You were wiggling like a nervous worm. I couldn't balance you right."

For a moment, the two dancers glared at each other. Nancy could feel the tension between them. She didn't dare say anything, especially when she had no idea what had caused the near-accident.

"I think we both know what the solution to all of this is," Lawrence said in a low voice. "Get yourself a new partner, one you can blame all your mistakes on." Then he turned and started toward the door.

"You know there's no one else around who can

44

partner me," Shana yelled after him. "So we'll just have to simplify the choreography for you."

"For me?" Lawrence halted. "Give it up, Shana. This whole thing was your own fault. Your timing was off. You're not nearly as good as you think you are. *Both* your sisters can dance circles around you, even Michelle. Darci should be dancing the Sugar Plum Fairy role, and you know it."

With that, Lawrence pushed his way through the doors and stormed out of the studio.

"Pompous jerk," Shana muttered as she sat down on the wooden floor. Ripping off her satin toe shoes, she flung them after him. "He makes me so mad!" she declared, tearing the lambswool padding from her toes and throwing it after her shoes.

Nancy had never seen Shana so worked up. Maybe the tense atmosphere at the ballet academy was getting to everyone. "Don't you two get along?" Nancy asked in a teasing voice, hoping to break the tension.

Shana gave Nancy a wry grin. "That's an understatement," she said with a sigh. "Actually, we used to be um . . . friends. I mean, before I got an audition with the New York Ballet Company and he didn't."

"Jealousy again," George remarked to Nancy in a low voice. Then she picked up Shana's toe shoes and handed them to her.

"Mmm," Nancy replied, thinking of Darci.

Shana walked over to the piano and punched off the tape recorder. The romantic *Nutcracker* music stopped. Then she gathered up her sweats and shawl.

Finally she said, "You know, Lawrence thinks I could arrange an audition for him with the New York Ballet Company if I really wanted to. But, I'm just a member of the corps de ballet right now—which means I'm not much more important than a piece of scenery. Lawrence doesn't understand that I have no say in who gets to audition and who doesn't." Wearily, Shana slumped onto the piano bench.

"Would you arrange an audition for Lawrence if you could?" Nancy pressed.

Shana shook her head as she tucked her toe shoes into her dance bag. Then she bent down to slip on her sweats. "No, he needs to do that himself. Lawrence has to have more confidence in his own abilities. It's the only way he'll make it in New York. The competition is cutthroat, and you've got to be able to deal with it—on your own."

"Do you think Lawrence knows how you feel?" Nancy asked.

"I know he knows, because I told him," Shana said. "Someone had to. He's fooling himself if he thinks a recommendation from me would make a difference. Blaming me is just a cop-out."

"Makes sense," George said, nodding. "Do you think Lawrence was mad enough to have taken screws out of the demonstration barre so you'd fall?"

"No way." Shana tucked an errant wisp of flame-red hair back in her loosened chignon and shook her head emphatically. But then her green eyes took on a faraway look. "At least I'd hate to think he'd do something like that," she said finally. "Not to me."

While Shana was talking, Nancy walked over to the studio doors and peered into the hall. She wanted to make sure no one was listening to them.

When she returned, she sat down next to Shana on the bench. "Maybe we'd better tell you about the other things that have happened," Nancy said in a low voice. Then she and George told her about the missing antique ornaments and the canceled programs.

"Poor Madame Dugrand," Shana murmured when Nancy had finished. "But what could those things have to do with the demonstration barre falling, or with Lawrence almost dropping me?"

"Maybe nothing," Nancy admitted. "But I can't help thinking they're all tied together."

"And you suspect Lawrence?" Shana shook her head. "I don't know, Nancy. Lawrence might be mad at me for a lot of things, but he's devoted to Madame Dugrand. I doubt he'd hurt her just to get back at me."

"Maybe we should tell Shana what we overheard at Yogurt Heaven, Nancy," George said in a low voice.

"What?" Shana looked back and forth at her two friends.

Reluctantly, Nancy repeated the conversation they'd overheard between Darci and Lawrence.

But Shana didn't seem angry. Instead she let out a sigh. "I should have known this would happen. Poor Darci. She wanted to be the Sugar Plum Fairy so badly. She's had to dance in my shadow all her life. Besides, Darci has a huge crush on Lawrence. My dancing with him must really burn her up."

"So you don't think they've teamed up to drive you away?" Nancy asked.

Shana shrugged. "I don't know anything anymore. I thought I was coming back to help Madame out, but it's been one disaster after another. Maybe I should just go back to New York."

"No way!" George said firmly. "Look at all the help you've given the other dancers. Madame needs you."

"Maybe." Shana stood up. "Well, I have to get going. Madame wants me to help choreograph the fight scene between the soldiers and the mice."

"How's your ankle?" Nancy asked, getting up.

Shana smiled. "All better, thanks to the ice pack. Look, you guys," she added as the three of them walked to the door, "I'm going to talk to Darci the first chance I get."

"Don't tell her I'm snooping around," Nancy

cautioned. "I don't think it'd be a good idea to blow my cover."

"I'll be careful," Shana promised. "I really appreciate what you're trying to do, Nancy. I don't know if I could stick around here at all under the circumstances if it weren't for you."

Nancy opened the door, and the three walked out of the studio. In the hall, a group of ten- and eleven-year-old boys and girls were battling with swords.

"They must be the mice and soldiers," George said. "That battle holds special memories for Nancy, Bess, and me," she told Shana.

Shana joined in the laughter. "I remember that scene. You three almost brought the tree down. *The Nutcracker* has never been quite as exciting. Well, I'd better get moving. I'll see you two later."

While Nancy and George worked their way around the battling kids to get to the prop room, Shana headed in the opposite direction.

George opened the prop room door. Nancy was about to step inside when Lawrence Steele came charging out. Bumping into Nancy, he knocked her against the door frame.

"Hey, Steele!" George said, catching Nancy by the arm. "Watch where you're going!"

"I might say the same thing to you," Lawrence countered. He raked his thick, blond hair back with his fingers. "What're you guys doing here, anyway? Snooping around?"

49

"I'm the prop mistress," Nancy announced.

Lawrence snorted. "That's a good one. Mrs. Patterson is in charge of props."

"Not anymore. She quit," Nancy retorted, tired of his haughty tone. "So what were *you* doing in the prop room?"

Lawrence hesitated, then shrugged. "I was looking for the Mouse King headpiece. They need it for rehearsal. It's not in the wardrobe room with the rest of the costumes, and Mrs. Wolaski thought it might have been put in here by mistake."

Glancing at Lawrence's empty hands, Nancy asked, "But it wasn't?"

"No," he replied. "At least, not that I could see. If you should stumble across it while straightening up that mess," he added, "bring it down to the wardrobe room." Then, not bothering to wait for a response, Lawrence continued down the hall.

"Oooo," George said, her dark eyes narrowing. "He sure can be a pain."

"I guess everyone has lost their sense of humor around here," Nancy agreed as they walked into the prop room. "That means we have to stay cool if we're going to get anywhere in this investigation."

When they got inside, George surveyed the room. "I have to agree with him about the mess part," she said.

"Mmmm. And before we leave this afternoon, I have to make sure those ornaments aren't here,"

Nancy told George. Nodding toward a stack of boxes on the other side of the prop room, she added, "I'll check those last boxes over there. Maybe you can start tagging scenery."

Taking a pad of paper and a magic marker, George walked over to a pair of large, white pillars. She gave one of them a little push. "They look like heavy wood," she said with a smile, "but they're just lightweight papier-mâché. They must be for the Land of Sweets."

Nancy nodded. "Maybe we should move them out of the way, so I can reach those other boxes." She walked over to help George.

"I'll push from behind," George suggested. "You stay in front and keep it from falling forward."

The girls were able to move the pillar about a foot before it began to topple.

"Be careful," Nancy said. "We don't want it to fall over."

As she and George steadied the pillar, Nancy looked up. The ceiling was so dark, she couldn't see very well. But when she stepped back she saw something that startled her. Perched on the top of the pillar was a wooden doll. It grinned down at her with a sinister smile.

"George, stop!" Nancy cried as the three-foot-tall doll began to teeter on the edge of the pillar.

But Nancy's warning came too late. The doll toppled from the column—heading straight for George's head!

6

Staged for Trouble

Nancy grabbed George by the hand and pulled her sideways. The wooden doll crashed to the floor at the base of the pillar, missing George's head by an inch. Losing her balance, George fell backward, landing on her rear in the floor of the sled.

"George!" Nancy hurried to her friend. "Are you all right?"

"I'm fine," George assured Nancy. Then she nodded toward the grinning doll, which was now lying on the floor, its head at an odd angle. "But I'm afraid he's not."

Nancy looked over at the fallen doll. "It's the nutcracker," Nancy said. "You know, the toy that Clara's godfather gives her in the first act." She bent down to pick up the doll's head. The brightly painted face with its smiling mouthful of teeth looked even more sinister without its body.

"Looks as if we're going to have to get another one, doesn't it?" George said.

Suddenly, the prop room door flew open. "What's going on in here?" It was Lawrence, followed by several young dancers, some in soldier costumes, others in tutus. Nancy recognized Michelle Edwards, Shana's ten-year-old sister, who was playing the part of Clara.

"Nothing," Nancy said, looking pointedly at Lawrence. "We're just trying to find all the props."

"My nutcracker!" Michelle wailed when she saw the broken head in Nancy's hands.

"Oh, great," Lawrence grumbled as he stepped toward the pillar. "One more thing around here to fix." Stooping, he picked up the doll's body and studied it.

Nancy thought Lawrence seemed more annoyed than surprised. He had just been in the prop room. Had he booby-trapped the pillar, hoping to scare or even hurt Nancy or George?

"Can you fix it, Lawrence?" Michelle asked anxiously.

Lawrence stood up. "Sure." He smiled and patted Michelle's head. "Now go on back to the studio. I'll join you there in a minute." When Michelle and the soldiers had gone, Lawrence turned to Nancy and George.

"You two had better be more careful," he said in a low voice. Then, tossing the nutcracker's body to Nancy, he added with a chuckle, "You wouldn't want to lose your head like this poor fellow, would you?"

Neither Nancy nor George thought his remark was funny. "We could have been hurt," Nancy said. "Someone deliberately set the doll on top of the pillar."

Lawrence frowned. "Do me a favor and leave the nutcracker in Madame Dugrand's office, okay? I'll take it home tonight and fix it." With that, he turned and strode from the room.

Holding out her hand to George, Nancy helped her friend out of the sled. "Do you think he was threatening us when he said we should be careful?" George asked.

"I don't know," Nancy said, picking up the nutcracker doll and placing it in the seat of the sled. "Lawrence could easily have been putting the nutcracker doll on top of the pillar while he was in here instead of looking for the Mouse King headpiece."

Just then the prop room door flew open once more. Nancy spun around, expecting to see Lawrence again.

It was Bess. "Lunchtime!" she announced cheerfully. "Actually, it's way past lunchtime. I'm starved."

"And we're swamped," Nancy waved her arm at all the opened boxes. "Lunch will have to wait."

"How about if I go to Yogurt Heaven and bring something back?" Bess offered.

"Great idea." Nancy pulled her car keys out of her purse and threw them to Bess.

When Bess had gone, George surveyed the room and groaned. "So where were we?"

Nancy laughed. "Still looking for the ornaments, I'm afraid. If I don't find them, I'll have to bring some from home. Maybe I can dress them up a bit with glitter and lace."

"That sounds like a lot of work," George said with a sigh. "Harder work than cross-country skiing."

About twenty minutes later, Bess called, "I'm back!" She was carrying bags of food. "Lunch, anyone?"

"I'm famished," George declared, dropping her marker and paper.

"Me, too," Nancy agreed. She took the car keys from Bess and stuck them in her pocket. Her fingers touched the fabric of the handkerchief she'd found earlier on the stage.

"We'll have a picnic." Bess set the food on a box, then pulled up another box to sit on. "It'll just be the three of us, though. Mrs. Wolaski was too busy to join us. That lady works like a beaver. I think she took only one break this morning."

Nancy held up the lacy handkerchief. "Look what I found backstage. It's a handkerchief with the initials *G. T.* embroidered on it. Does anyone here have those initials, Bess?"

Bess thought for a moment, then shrugged. "I don't know. Why?"

"G. T. might just know something about the missing ornaments or the fire," Nancy said. "I think I'll ask Madame Dugrand if she knows who it belongs to."

"Madame isn't here," Bess said, taking a bite of her sandwich. "She was going out as I was coming in. She said something about seeing the printers about the programs."

Nancy tucked the handkerchief back into the pocket of her jeans, then joined George and Bess. "I'll ask Madame about it tomorrow, then."

Bess was about to take a sip of her drink when she noticed the nutcracker doll on the seat of the sled. Her eyes widened and she made a face. "What *is* that thing staring at me?"

"The nutcracker," George replied. "Someone stuck him on top of the pillar, and when Nancy and I moved it, the doll fell down on us."

"Weird." Bess shook her head and shivered slightly.

Nancy paused before biting into her tuna roll. "I hope there aren't any more booby traps in here."

"Booby traps?" Bess repeated, looking around nervously. "Are you saying someone deliberately planted that doll up there so it would fall?"

"Not someone," George corrected. "Lawrence."

"We don't know that for sure, George," Nancy cautioned. "Who knows? It could be G. T., whoever that is."

Standing up, Bess moved her box closer to

Nancy's. "I think I've lost my appetite," she said. "Or maybe it's the way that thing is watching me," she added, glancing over at the nutcracker.

George started to giggle. "It's just a *doll*, Bess." Reaching into the sled, she turned the nutcracker head over so its face was hidden. Even Nancy had to admit she was glad the nutcracker was no longer looking at them.

Nancy and Bess arrived early at the dance school on Saturday morning. Bess headed straight for the wardrobe room. Nancy took the box of ornaments she'd found in her attic at home to the prop room. The ornaments wouldn't exactly pass for antiques, but with a little dressing up, they'd work fine. Setting down the box, Nancy went back down the hall to talk to Madame Dugrand.

"Come in," Madame called when Nancy knocked on her office door.

The directress was sitting at her desk, a bright smile on her face. "I have good news, Nancy. The programs will be ready Wednesday morning after all. Now I can relax and have a good time at the gala tonight."

She sounded so happy and relieved that Nancy decided not to mention Mrs. Farnsworth's missing ornaments until after the party.

"I'm looking forward to the gala, too," Nancy told the directress.

Madame stood up. "So, what can I do for you?"

"Has anyone mentioned losing a handkerchief?" Nancy asked, taking the lacy square of fabric from her pocket. "I found this yesterday."

Madame took the handkerchief from Nancy and examined it for a moment before handing it back. "G. T." The directress murmured, then shook her head. "I'm afraid I don't know anyone with those initials."

"Would you mind if I took a look at the current class list?" Nancy asked.

"Of course not." Madame took a piece of paper out of her desk drawer. "But why are you so interested?"

Nancy hesitated as she looked over the list. She didn't want to alarm Madame unnecessarily. "I found the handkerchief backstage. Near the curtain where the fire started."

Madame's brows raised in concern. "Do you think the person who started the fire may have dropped the handkerchief?"

"It's possible." Nancy gave the list back to the directress. There was no one on it with the initials *G. T.*

Madame frowned. "I'm sure it was just a careless student—or parent. It must have been someone who knows how strict I am about smoking, so the person hid backstage."

"You're probably right," Nancy said, nodding. "I'll hang on to this, if you don't mind." She slipped the handkerchief back into her pocket. "Maybe someone will come looking for it." With that, Nancy excused herself and returned to the prop room.

For the next two hours, Nancy worked on dressing up the shiny glass balls she'd brought from home with glitter, lace, and sequins. She had just decided to take a break when she heard music coming from the recital hall. Walking to the door that led to the backstage area, Nancy quietly opened it and peeked up the stairs.

Madame Dugrand, Darci, Lawrence, and several of the older students were on stage. It was obviously a rehearsal, and Nancy thought it would be fun to watch for a few minutes. Slipping into the room, she headed toward the front row of seats in the recital hall and sat down.

"I want you to dance the pas de deux full out," Madame Dugrand told Lawrence. "Where's Shana?"

"Over here," Shana said, entering from offstage. Madame Dugrand went to the side of the stage to rewind the tape. While the directress's back was turned, Nancy saw Shana shoot Lawrence an apprehensive look. Nancy could hardly blame her after the near-accident the day before.

Lawrence raised his brows as if to say, "So what's your problem?" Immediately, Shana's apprehensive look turned into an icy glare.

Nancy looked around for Darci. Shana's younger sister had melted into the shadows of the backstage curtain. The other students were talking quietly, but Darci stood with folded arms, her green eyes riveted on Lawrence and Shana.

If Madame Dugrand noticed the tension in the air, she gave no indication. As soon as she had the tape player going, she walked to the front of the stage and clapped her hands. Shana and Lawrence found their marks, the places on the stage where they were to stand when the dance started.

At first, the couple moved hesitantly, as if they were afraid to touch each other. But as the music continued, it seemed to cast its spell on the two of them, and they began to move in synchronized harmony.

When it was time for the difficult lift that Lawrence had flubbed the day before, Nancy held her breath. This time, however, he raised his graceful partner with ease. As he turned slowly with Shana high above his head, Madame Dugrand and the other dancers applauded . . . all but Darci Edwards.

With an angry frown, Shana's sister threw her towel around her shoulders and stomped offstage. Then, she leaped down the stage steps and stormed up the aisle of the recital hall, banging the doors behind her.

"Bravo! Very nice!" Madame declared, smiling approvingly as Lawrence set Shana down. Still clapping, the other students came forward and surrounded the couple. Suddenly, Nancy realized that it was starting to snow onstage—not just a few flakes, but a regular blizzard.

"What on earth?" Madame looked up as a blur of snowflakes fluttered from offstage.

"It's the snow machine!" one of the students yelled.

"Well, someone turn it off!" Throwing her hands into the air, Madame started forward.

"I'll do it," Lawrence said quickly.

By then, a thin layer of "snow" had begun to accumulate onstage.

"I can't believe this," said Madame, shaking her head. "What else is going to go wrong?"

Lawrence hurried across the stage. Suddenly, his feet slipped out from under him. Lurching sideways, he fell into Madame Dugrand, knocking her backward.

With a gasp, Nancy jumped up. "Madame!" she cried. But it was too late. The directress flew off the stage, dropping several feet to the floor of the recital hall!

7

Big Preparations

Nancy rushed to Madame's side. The directress was sprawled on the wooden floor, her arms and legs jutting out at odd angles. Her eyes were closed. Lawrence jumped from the stage and kneeled next to Nancy.

When Nancy looked up, she saw Shana and the other dancers staring from the edge of the stage, concerned expressions on their faces. Behind them, snow continued to fall onto the stage floor.

"Don't move her," Nancy cautioned. "Shana, call nine-one-one."

"Wait," Lawrence said as Madame's lids began to flutter open. "Madame, are you all right?"

Madame stared up at him. "Yes," she replied, sounding dazed. "What happened? What am I doing here?" she asked, struggling up on her elbows.

Nancy put her hands gently on the directress's shoulders. "Madame," she said. "Please don't move. You might have broken something."

"Nonsense." Madame sat up and gave her arms a shake.

Lawrence gently checked Madame's knees and calves. Holding her ankle up, he rotated first one foot, and then the other. "Any pain?" he asked.

Madame shook her head. "I'm fine," she said. "Now help me up," she added, holding out her hand to Lawrence. "After twenty-five years of training as a ballerina I think I'd know if I was hurt."

Taking the directress's hand, Lawrence lifted her to her feet. Supporting Madame's other arm, Nancy stood up next to her.

"What happened, anyway?" Madame asked as she brushed off her long skirt.

"Ask Lawrence," a low voice said, in an accusing tone. Nancy looked up at the stage. Shana was staring down at them, her hands on her hips. Her green eyes snapped angrily and her lips were pressed in a thin line. "Lawrence bumped into you on purpose and knocked you off the stage," Shana said.

Madame's eyes widened in shock. "Shana! What a terrible thing to say."

"It was an accident!" Lawrence protested, glaring up at Shana. "I slipped on the snow."

"That's a likely story," Shana retorted. "You've danced plenty of times in the snow."

"This stuff *is* pretty slimy," one of the dancers declared. She'd scooped up some of the white flakes and was rubbing it between her fingers.

Moving to the edge of the stage, Nancy ran her hand through the snow, then held her finger to her nose and smelled it.

"It's soap," she announced.

Madame Dugrand scooped up some of the flakes herself. "It *is* soap," she agreed. "How did that happen? The snow machine is suppose to blow out tiny bits of paper. They shouldn't be slippery at all."

"Who fills the snow machine?" Nancy asked.

"That's one of Lawrence's jobs," Madame replied.

All eyes turned back to Lawrence.

"Wait a minute!" He held up his hands in protest.

"Quit acting so innocent, Lawrence Steele!" Shana waved an angry finger at him. "Why don't you just admit you put soap flakes in the snow machine before rehearsal? You probably wanted *me* to fall!"

"Hey, *I* almost fell," Lawrence pointed out. "Why would I want to hurt myself?"

Madame clapped her hands to her ears. "Stop! Stop all of this bickering."

Lawrence and Shana shut their mouths immediately and stared at Madame. Taking her hands off her ears, the directress said calmly, "Now, let's get the stage cleaned up. We have a show to rehearse."

As Nancy followed Lawrence up the stage steps, she wondered if Darci had turned on the snow machine. Nancy remembered how Shana's younger sister had stormed out of the recital hall seconds before the flakes had started spewing through the air.

But anyone could have filled the machine with soap earlier, Nancy realized—including Lawrence.

Several students came back onstage carrying brooms, dustpans, and buckets. As Nancy bent down to scrape snow onto a dustpan, she heard Shana speaking to Madame in a low voice.

Nancy looked over her shoulder. Shana and the directress were standing offstage, directly behind her. "I won't dance with him again," Nancy heard Shana say.

Madame only closed her eyes tiredly. "Go home, Shana," she said. "Get ready for the gala. We'll all relax and enjoy ourselves tonight, and forget this little incident ever happened."

"I won't forget," Shana muttered, and snatching up her dance bag, she stomped toward the exit.

Lawrence and the other students watched her go. Lawrence's face was flushed, and he looked genuinely upset. Nancy shook her head. Shana's behavior wasn't helping things. Whoever was trying to sabotage Madame Dugrand's production of *The Nutcracker* was doing a good job of it.

Nancy wished she was closer to cracking the case. What she definitely needed to do was question Darci Edwards, though she had a feeling the young dancer would tell her to mind her own business.

With a sigh, Nancy finished cleaning the stage and went back into the prop room. She found her coat, then left to find Bess. Maybe talking to her friend would help her sort things out.

"I sent Bess upstairs to get some tape," Mrs. Wolaski said when Nancy arrived downstairs.

In front of the wardrobe mistress, Michelle Edwards was standing on a stool. Mrs. Wolaski was bent over, pinning the hem of Michelle's Clara costume, an old-fashioned dress with short, puffy sleeves and a wide green sash. When Michelle smiled down at Nancy, she looked just like her older sister, Shana.

Nancy found another stool and sat down. "I'll wait here for her."

"How is my nutcracker doll, Nancy?" asked Michelle from her high perch.

"I don't know. Lawrence has it," Nancy said.

"If Lawrence has it, it's all right," Michelle said confidently.

"All set." Mrs. Wolaski straightened slowly. "You can take the dress off now, dear. When you come back on Monday, we'll fit it again."

Michelle jumped from the stool and pulled the ruffled gown over her head. She was wearing her leotard underneath.

"Michelle," Bess said as she came into the room, "your mother is upstairs, waiting for you. It's time to go home and get ready for the gala."

"Yippee!" Michelle cried excitedly, and scampered off.

"Did you get the tape, Bess?" Mrs. Wolaski asked.

"Madame said she'd get it for you tomorrow," Bess explained. "She seemed kind of distracted."

Mrs. Wolaski gave her small round glasses a poke. "Poor Alicia. She's always so overwhelmed. Oh, well. Would you mind taking the Clara gown home with you to hem, Bess?"

"I'd be glad to," Bess said. Then, turning to Nancy, she asked, "What on earth just happened, Nancy? Do you know? Everyone seems upset."

"The snow machine suddenly went on during a rehearsal," Nancy told her. "It was loaded with soap flakes, and Lawrence slipped. He knocked Madame off the stage."

"My goodness!" Mrs. Wolaski exclaimed. "Is Alicia all right?"

Nancy nodded. "She got right up."

Mrs. Wolaski shook her head and sighed. "It's always something, isn't it?"

"Let's hope the gala will make everyone feel better," Bess said. "I know I'm looking forward to it."

"Are you going to the gala, Mrs. Wolaski?" Nancy asked.

"Oh, no. Once I get home at night, I'm always too tired to think of going out again."

Bess grabbed her coat. "Oh, Mrs. Wolaski, you really should go. Remember the saying, "All work and no play . . .""

". . . makes you very tired at the end of the day," Mrs. Wolaski chuckled. Then she rubbed her back. "No, I think soaking in a hot bath sounds like fun to me."

"Well, if you change your mind, we'll be glad to pick you up," Nancy said.

"You're both very sweet," Mrs. Wolaski replied. "Now go and have a good time for me."

The girls said goodbye, then Nancy took Bess home. As soon as she got home herself, Nancy showered and changed into her new turquoise party dress and black patent leather heels.

Half an hour later, Nancy was parking her Mustang in front of Bess's house.

"Come in, Nancy," Mrs. Marvin said as she opened the door. "Bess is just about ready."

"I'm totally ready," Bess said, hurrying down the stairs in her bright red brocade dress and matching leather flats.

"When will you girls be home?" Mrs. Marvin asked as Bess was putting on her coat.

"We shouldn't be too late," Bess replied. The girls said goodbye and headed for Nancy's car.

"Would you mind stopping off at the dance academy on the way to the country club, Nancy?" Bess asked. "I forgot to bring Michelle's Clara costume home with me, and I'm supposed to do the hem."

"Sure," Nancy said. "We're a little early, anyway."

Nancy turned down Mason Street, then pulled into the dance school's parking lot. It was dark, and the only other vehicle in sight was the school van, which was parked in its usual place at the back of the lot.

"I don't think anyone's here," Nancy said. "How did you plan to get in?"

"I've got a key," Bess said. She opened her black evening bag and took it out. "Mrs. Wolaski loaned it to me yesterday, and I forgot to give it back."

Nancy pulled the Mustang to the end of the front sidewalk and parked. Giggling, the two girls held on to each other as they inched their way up the icy walk to the school in their dress shoes. Once inside the door, Nancy was about to turn on the lights when she heard a noise coming from down the hall.

"Did you hear that?" she whispered to Bess.

Bess nodded. "I sure did!"

"I'm going to check it out. Wait here," Nancy said, slipping out of her heels.

"No way," Bess said, taking off her own party shoes. "I'm going with you."

Nancy tiptoed down the shadowy hall in her stockinged feet. The hall was dimly lit by the weak glow of an emergency light. Nancy could hear Bess breathing as she followed just behind her.

Nancy stopped in front of the recital room door and put a finger to her lips. The girls listened first at the door to studio A. Then they heard a crash from the prop room.

Bess jumped. "What was that?" she squealed,

clutching Nancy's arm. "I think we'd better call the police."

Nancy shook her head emphatically. "If we wait for the police," she whispered, "whoever it is might get away."

Bess grimaced, then nodded reluctantly. Nancy hurried to the prop room. Slowly, she pushed open the door and peered inside cautiously. It was pitch black.

Stepping into the room, Nancy felt along the brick wall for the light switch. Bess was so close behind her that she kept stepping on Nancy's heels.

"Grrrr!" A loud growl made Nancy swing around. Bess screamed as a black shape jumped up from behind the shadowy sled.

Bess screamed again as the creature lunged for the door. In the dim light from the hall, Nancy could see it had a huge head and pointy ears.

"A monster! And it's coming after us!" Bess cried, shrinking back against Nancy.

"Stop, whoever you are!" Nancy pushed past Bess, trying to reach the creature. But her leg hit something solid and she tumbled over a box. At the same time, the monster bolted past her and out into the hall.

Bess helped Nancy struggle to her feet. "We can't let it get away!" she yelled, but Bess just stood frozen in fear.

Nancy leaped toward the open door. *Wham!* It slammed shut in her face. Quickly, she searched for the door knob, but then she heard a click.

With a sinking feeling, Nancy turned the knob, then rattled it. Nothing happened. The door was locked.

She could hear Bess gasp. "Don't move," Nancy whispered to her friend. "I need to find the light." Groping along the wall beside the door, Nancy finally located the light switch. When she flipped it on, nothing happened. Someone had turned off the power. Nancy and Bess were locked in a pitch black room!

8

In the Lair of the Mouse King

"What in the world was that?" Bess finally asked, from beside Nancy.

"Believe it or not, I think it was the Mouse King," Nancy said, looking around. The prop room was so dark, it was like being in a cave. And because she knew the floor was littered with junk, she didn't dare take a step.

Bess laughed nervously. "The Mouse King? You're kidding. Who would be crazy enough to run around in a seven-headed mouse costume?"

"Someone who didn't want us to recognize him or her," Nancy replied. Mentally, she kicked herself. Like a dummy, she'd left her purse in the car. That meant she didn't have a flashlight or her lock-picking kit. She hated being so unprepared.

Bess let out her breath. "Well, I guess knowing that it was just a person wearing a costume makes me feel better."

Nancy gave a low chuckle. "At least something's making you feel better. Since we're locked in and the power is off, we may be in for a long night."

"It's a good thing we wore our coats. Hey, wait a minute. Aren't there two doors to this room?" Bess asked in a hopeful voice.

"You're right! How could I have forgotten that?" Nancy turned toward where she thought the backstage door was, but the total darkness was disorienting. "This place could be booby-trapped," she added, remembering how the nutcracker doll had nearly fallen on George's head. "Maybe the Mouse King was in here rigging up another surprise."

"Oh, great." Bess groaned.

Nancy was trying to decide what to do next when Bess suddenly grabbed her arm. "Nancy," she whispered, "do you hear squeaking?"

Nancy stopped to listen, then nodded. "Yes. And I'm pretty sure I know what it is."

"What?" Bess asked nervously.

"Don't panic, but it sounds like mice," Nancy said. "You know, those harmless little furry creatures."

"Mice!" Bess jumped toward Nancy, almost knocking her over. "Get me out of here!"

Suddenly, the prop room lights blazed on.

"That's weird," Nancy said, frowning.

Bess shivered. "Now I'll be able to *see* the little furry things instead of just hear them."

A few minutes later, a key turned in the lock and the door flew open.

"Caught you!" a voice cried. Whirling around, Nancy and Bess found themselves face to face with Lawrence Steele. He was brandishing a tire iron menacingly. When he saw Nancy and Bess, he raised his brows in puzzled surprise. "What are you two doing here?"

"Somebody locked us in," Nancy said simply. She looked at him suspiciously. "And what are you doing here?"

Lawrence snorted. "Saving your skin!" he retorted. "You would have spent a cold night in the prop room if I hadn't decided to drive by the school on my way to the gala. I saw that the front door was wide open, so I grabbed my tire iron and came in to take a look around. Then, when I tried the light in the hall, I figured someone had switched off the main breakers."

"I bet *you* locked us in here," Bess accused. Stepping forward, she glared up at the handsome dancer.

"Ha! Believe me, if I'd locked you in, I certainly wouldn't be stupid enough to let you out."

Bess shrugged. "I guess you're right," she said. "But then who did shut us in here?"

"Whoever the person was, he found your Mouse King headpiece," Nancy told Lawrence. "He put it on so we couldn't recognize him."

Suddenly, Bess let out a little shriek and jumped on top of a box.

"What's wrong with you?" Lawrence demanded, pointing at Bess with his tire iron. "And where are your shoes?" he added, looking at her stockinged feet.

"There are mice in here," Nancy explained. "We left our shoes by the door so the intruder wouldn't—"

"Mice!" Lawrence interrupted. He leaned the tire iron against the door jamb, then fell to his knees and began crawling around.

"Have you gone crazy?" Bess inquired as Lawrence crawled past her.

"Of course not," he snapped. "I'm looking for my mice."

"Your mice?" Bess repeated in disbelief.

Lawrence stopped to peer under the sled. "The mice in here must be the ones that were stolen from my locker a couple of days ago."

"You keep *mice* in your dance locker?" Bess stared down from the box, a horrified look on her face.

"Not usually. Only when I plan to feed my snake. Ah ha!" Lawrence said suddenly, pouncing on something. Getting to his feet, he held up a struggling white mouse by its pink tail.

Bess wrinkled her nose in disgust. "Yuck." Lawrence slipped the mouse into a pocket of his tweed top coat. Then he looked back and forth at Bess and Nancy. "Okay, so why don't you girls explain what you're doing in here?"

"We're just helping Madame," Nancy replied.

"Bess had to pick up a costume to hem, and we heard a noise. So we went to investigate, and . . ." Her voice trailed away.

Lawrence nodded. "And you figured it was me wearing a giant mouse head. I guess you don't seem to trust me very much, Ms. Drew."

Nancy raised her brows. "What makes you say that?" she asked in an innocent voice.

"Oh, it's just a feeling I get," Lawrence replied. He picked up the tire iron and slapped it against his left palm. "No one seems to believe in me these days," he added.

Before Nancy could reply, Bess put her hand on Nancy's shoulder and jumped off the box. "Well, you did almost drop Shana on her head," she pointed out.

"That was Shana's fault," Lawrence said. "She's trying to ruin my career."

Before Nancy could stop her, Bess said, "We happen to know that *you're* the one who's trying to get rid of *her*."

"Look, another mouse," Nancy cut in quickly, pointing at the floor behind Lawrence. "It just ran under the cannon."

"Excellent!" Lawrence dropped to his knees again, and the two girls hurried quietly out the prop room door.

"Let's get out of here quick," Bess said, skidding down the hall after Nancy. "That guy with his mice is nuts."

Nancy stopped at the end of the hall. "I should probably look around first," she said. "If Lawrence is telling the truth, then the person we surprised in the prop room might still be in the building somewhere."

"No way." Bess tugged on Nancy's coat sleeve. "'Cause if Lawrence is lying, he'll be after us in two seconds."

"You're right." Nancy headed toward the front door. Suddenly, lights from outside the building briefly flooded the hallway.

"Headlights!" Nancy exclaimed. She rushed to the door just in time to see the school van roar out of the parking lot.

"Do you think Lawrence is making a getaway?" Bess asked.

Quickly, Nancy slipped her high heels back on, then started outside. "I don't know," she replied, "but we need to find out. It could be the person who was wearing the Mouse King headpiece."

"If we go after the van, we'll miss the gala!" Bess protested, struggling into her red flats. But Nancy was already heading down the steps to the car. Slipping and sliding on the ice, she made her way to the Mustang.

"Wait for me!" Bess called. She was shuffling carefully along the snowy walk, trying not to fall.

Nancy jumped into the car and started the engine. Reaching across the passenger seat, she opened the door for Bess. "Hurry!" she urged.

As soon as Bess had climbed in and strapped on her seatbelt, Nancy pushed the gas pedal to the floor. She wanted to catch whoever was driving the van—or at least find out where he or she was going.

"Oh, no." Bess was bent over in her seat. "Look at my stockings. They're ruined!"

"Mmmm," Nancy commented without really hearing her friend. She was trying to spot the white van. Suddenly, she saw it make a left turn several cars ahead. "There it is!" she cried, wheeling the Mustang abruptly into the left lane.

Bess grabbed for the dashboard. "Can you see who's driving?"

Nancy shook her head. "Too far away."

Just then fat, wet snowflakes began to hit the windshield. "Oh, great," Nancy groaned as she flipped on the wipers. "Just what we don't need. Brace yourself, Bess, I'm turning."

With both hands tight on the steering wheel, Nancy made a sharp left. The snow was falling faster, and it was hard to see out the window.

"Did we lose the van?" Bess asked.

"Let's hope not." Nancy checked out the side window. "Can you tell where we are?"

"Yeah," Bess replied. "It's that new apartment complex. You know, the one they advertise as having Jacuzzis, a health club, and an indoor pool."

Nancy thought for a minute as the Mustang cruised down the street. There were three apartment complexes on each side. "Who from the dance school would have a place here?" she mused.

"My guess would be Lawrence," Bess replied. "But I think this place is pretty expensive."

Glancing out the window again, Nancy noted that each complex consisted of four apartment buildings built around a central court. In the middle of the court was a pool and some kind of recreation room. The apartment buildings themselves were three levels high, with fancy balconies overlooking the pool.

"They do look pretty nice." Nancy stopped the car at the end of the main thoroughfare. "So where did the van go? There's no way out."

Bess turned in her seat to look at Nancy. "I think we've been led on a wild goose chase."

"Maybe." Nancy turned the Mustang around and headed back to the main street. "Still, tomorrow I'm going to check all the addresses of people associated with the dance school. We may just get lucky."

Suddenly, as Nancy drove past the second complex on the right, she heard the roar of a motor close behind them. She looked in the rearview mirror, but the rear windshield was covered with heavy snow.

Then she heard another roar. Something smacked the Mustang's rear bumper so hard that Nancy and Bess were both thrown forward.

Bess's eyes widened. "Someone's crashing into us!" she cried fearfully.

"Hold on," Nancy said in a low voice. She rolled down her window and shot a look over her shoulder. The white van was about fifteen feet behind them. Almost immediately, its motor roared as it headed after them again.

Sticking her head back inside, Nancy stepped on the gas, hoping to shoot out of the van's path. But as she did, the Mustang's back wheels spun in the slippery dusting of snow on the street, and the car fishtailed forward. Quickly, Nancy wiped off the side mirror. The van was swerving after them, as if its driver were determined not to let them get away.

Suddenly, Bess sat up straight in her seat. "Nancy, stop!" she screamed. "We're headed for the intersection!"

Nancy hit the brakes hard. At the same time, she heard the crunch of bumper against bumper as the van rammed them from behind. The force sent the Mustang skidding forward, through the red light and straight into traffic!

9

A Gala Event

"We're going to crash!" Bess threw her arms in front of her face and screamed as the Mustang skated sideways into the intersection. Horns honked and tires screeched.

Nancy took her foot off the brake, remembering her dad's advice about driving in the snow— slamming on the brakes would only make the car fishtail like crazy. Still, Nancy knew Bess was right. There was no way they were going to get through the intersection without an accident.

Crunch! The Mustang hit something hard and jolted to a stop. Nancy's head snapped back and her seatbelt dug into her chest. But when she looked around, she saw with relief that Bess and the car seemed to be all right. We probably hit a curb, Nancy thought with relief.

Bess was staring at her in amazement. "We're still in one piece," she said in a shaky voice.

Nancy nodded slowly. "I think we made it."

"Whew." Bess's shoulders slumped and she buried her head in her hands. "Remind me never to go to a demolition derby. I've been in one already."

A rapping sound on the window made Nancy look up. A police officer was staring in at them, his brows furrowed with concern. Snow covered his police hat. "Are you ladies all right? That was quite a wild ride across the intersection."

"We're fine," Nancy replied. "Was anyone hurt?"

The officer shook his head. "Believe it or not, it appears that we have just a couple of dented fenders."

Bess leaned forward. "It wasn't her fault, Officer," she said. "A van rammed us from behind."

"We know. Lucky for you, a witness saw the van hit you, then take off. They even gave us a license number. My partner's calling it in."

"We already know who the van belongs to," Nancy said grimly.

"A jealous boyfriend?" the officer guessed as he pulled out a pad.

Nancy shook her head. "The van belongs to Madame Dugrand's Dance Academy on Mason Street. We think the person driving it broke into the school."

The policeman stopped writing. "Hmmm. This is serious. Let me see what my partner found out. Then we'll fill out an accident report."

When the officer had left, Nancy opened the

car door and walked to the front of the Mustang. Luckily, the car had only collided with the curb opposite the entrance to the apartment complex. The two side tires were crunched against the concrete. It looked as if she would still be able to drive it. Nancy was thankful they hadn't been going very fast when the van rammed them.

"Is the car okay?" Bess called.

"I guess we lucked out." Nancy glanced at the intersection. Fortunately, the Mustang was far enough off the road so that traffic could move around it. On the other side of the street were the two police cars, their red lights flashing. In the middle of the intersection three cars were piled into each other. A cluster of people had gathered around them.

Nancy grimaced. "Those must be the drivers who had to brake to avoid us."

"We should go over and thank them," Bess said.

"That's for sure." Nancy shut her car door, then walked around to Bess's side. "Then, after we make out our accident report, I'd like to go back to the dance academy. The culprit may have ditched the van back there."

Bess sighed. "I should have known you'd say that. I guess I don't feel much like going to the gala anymore anyway. I mean, look at my stockings and shoes," she added, glancing down at her snow-caked flats and the runs that striped her stockings.

"It is getting late," Nancy said as she walked to

the edge of the road. Traffic was light, but the snow was still falling steadily. "We're still going to the gala, though, Bess, so start getting in the party mood." Nancy looked both ways, then sprinted across the road, calling over her shoulder, "I wouldn't miss it for anything!"

Half an hour later, Nancy and Bess pulled onto Mason Street. When the dance school was in sight, Nancy switched off the car lights.

Bess grasped Nancy's sleeve. "Look! The van!"

Nancy peered out the window. She could see the dim outline of the van through the snow. As she'd expected, the vehicle was parked in its regular spot. Nancy turned the Mustang into the parking lot and stopped about twenty feet behind the van. "We need to call the police," Bess said.

Nancy nodded. "You're right. But first I want to make sure our culprit's not here. This time he or she isn't getting away." With those words, Nancy flicked on the car lights. When they beamed into the back window of the van, they silhouetted a shape sitting on the passenger side.

"Somebody's in there!" Bess's voice shook.

Nancy opened the car door. "I'm going to take a closer look." Nancy pulled on her gloves. "I don't want to erase any clues. I'm sure the police will dust for prints. But I think I know who—or at least what—is in the van," she said grimly.

"Are you crazy?" Bess called after her.

Heart pounding, Nancy walked toward the van

and grabbed the handle of the passenger door. She pressed the knob, then quickly swung the door open. Immediately, a huge brown furry thing leaped out at her. Nancy gasped and jumped backward as the Mouse King headpiece fell to the snowy ground.

Nancy let out her breath. Her hunch had been correct. Gingerly picking the headpiece up, she carried it to the Mustang.

Bess rolled her window partway down. "Yuck! Don't you dare put that thing in here!"

"Be brave, Bess, because I don't have any other place to put it." Opening her door, Nancy threw the headpiece into the backseat. "I'm going to look around a bit."

Nancy walked back to the van. Right away she saw that a single pair of footprints led to the road from the driver's side. The prints were too small to belong to Lawrence but probably just right for Darci. Nancy followed the prints to the street, where the footsteps met up with another set of tire tracks. Whoever had been driving the van had been alone until they met someone in a car.

Nancy retraced her steps to the van. Bess was standing beside it, her arms wrapped around her chest. She was shivering. "I refuse to stay in the car with a giant mouse," she said.

Nancy laughed. "Then help me look around. I need to find out what the person was trying to do when we surprised him or her at the school." She walked quickly to the back of the van.

"Good question," Bess said, following Nancy. "But why did the person lead us into the apartment complex, then slam us from behind?"

Nancy shook her head. "It does seem kind of strange. I think he or she was just trying to scare us off." She tried the van's back double doors and found they weren't locked. Nancy peered inside the van. Except for a spare tire, it was empty.

Bess looked over her shoulder. "Well, if the Mouse King guy took something from the school, it's gone now."

Placing her hand carefully on the van door, Nancy hoisted herself into the back of the vehicle. Keeping low, she made her way to the other side of the spare tire, where a red glow caught her eye. When Nancy bent to look closer, she could see that the object was a smashed Christmas tree ornament.

Nancy held up a piece of the broken ball for Bess to see.

"Is that one of Mrs. Farnsworth's ornaments?" Bess asked in surprise.

"No, it's one of mine. I recognize the lace I glued around it," Nancy said, jumping from the van.

Bess furrowed her brow. "But why would anyone steal *your* ornaments?"

"Maybe our thieves just want to ruin the production any way they can," Nancy guessed as she shut the van doors. "But why would anyone chance breaking into the school tonight just to get some cheap ornaments? It seems awfully risky."

"Not that risky," Bess pointed out. "Whoever it was probably thought we were all going to be at the gala."

"You're right." Nancy hurried toward the Mustang. "We need to call the police, then get to the gala ourselves. We might just find out who else came late to the party!"

Fifteen minutes later, the girls pulled into the driveway of the River Heights Country Club. "If Darci and Lawrence aren't at the gala yet, we're definitely on the right track," Nancy said.

"And what if they've been here the whole time?" Bess asked.

"Then we'll have to do some serious detective work," Nancy replied as she stopped the car under the club's green awning. The parking valet appeared immediately to open the girls' doors.

When Nancy and Bess reached the main dining room where the party was taking place, they both stopped short in the doorway.

"Oh, Nancy!" Bess exclaimed. "It's the Land of Sweets."

The dining room was decorated to look like the enchanted land that Clara and her prince would visit in the second act of *The Nutcracker*. The support columns were wound with red and white crepe paper to look like candy canes. The walls had been decorated with paintings of gingerbread houses, glittery cupcakes, and cherrytopped sundaes. There were Christmas trees in the corners of the room, decked with candy canes and lollipops. Since the Land of Sweets was ruled by the Sugar Plum Fairy, and the gala was in Shana's honor, the decorations seemed particularly appropriate.

"Hi, Bess!" Michelle Edwards cried. "Isn't this fantastic?" Running up, she took Bess by the hands and danced her around in a circle.

With a laugh, Bess slowed, then reached down to hug her. "It's beautiful, and so are you with that gorgeous green dress on."

Michelle's face suddenly grew serious. "What took you so long? Shana thought you'd never get here."

Nancy looked quickly around the room. "Where is your sister?" she asked.

"She's over there," Michelle said, pointing to a pink ice sculpture of a ballerina. Shana stood in front of it, surrounded by a cluster of young dancers and their parents.

"And what about Darci?" Nancy asked.

Michelle looked surprised. "Darci? Oh, she wouldn't come."

"Darci's not here?" Nancy said, exchanging a meaningful glance with Bess.

"No." Michelle frowned. "Darci and Shana had a big fight before the gala. Darci locked herself in her room and wouldn't come out. She wouldn't even talk to Mom or Dad. We left for the gala without her."

Bingo, Nancy thought. Now she just had to find out about Lawrence.

"Come and look at all the food," Michelle urged. Grabbing Bess's hand, the young girl began to tug her across the floor.

"I'll see you in a minute," Bess called as Michelle pulled her toward a table full of cakes and cookies.

Nancy nodded and began to walk slowly through the crowd, searching for Lawrence. He was nowhere in sight.

"Nancy!" Shana cried when she caught sight of her friend. Excusing herself to her fans, the dancer hurried over to Nancy. She looked stunning in an off-the-shoulder midnight-blue satin sheath.

"Where have you been?" Shana asked. "All these kids and parents are driving me crazy."

"Uh, I'll tell you later," Nancy replied, looking over her shoulder. She could see Madame Dugrand talking to another group of people, gesturing dramatically. Nancy knew she'd have to find a moment alone with the directress soon, to tell her what had happened earlier in the evening.

"Where's Lawrence?" Nancy asked, turning back to Shana.

The redhead's cheeks flushed pink. "That jerk. He showed up for half an hour to charm everyone, and then he left, without any explanation."

"Do you know where he went?" Nancy pressed.

To Nancy's surprise, Shana suddenly looked as if she were about to cry. "Why don't you ask him yourself!" she said, nodding toward the entrance. Nancy whirled around. Lawrence was standing in the arched doorway, arm in arm with a triumphant-looking Darci!

10

A Sobbing Suspect

Nancy stared at the newcomers in the doorway. It appeared that Darci and Lawrence had just arrived—together. If so, then Nancy was sure the two of them could have been responsible for sabotaging *The Nutcracker* production. Nancy knew she'd have to find just the right time to confront them.

"Look at those two," Shana whispered. "Lawrence struts back in like a peacock, and Darci's got so much eye shadow on she looks like a raccoon. She's trying to look sophisticated."

Trying not to appear too obvious, Nancy studied the couple as they came into the room. Darci was wearing a short black knit dress that accented her creamy skin and chestnut hair. But her eyes were slightly puffy, as if she'd been crying.

Nancy swung her gaze to Lawrence. He looked even more handsome than usual, dressed in a navy sports coat and gray pants. Bowing his head right and left, he greeted all the smiling parents and giggling young girls.

"Really," Shana grumbled. "You'd think Lawrence was some kind of celebrity."

For a second, Nancy glanced back at Shana. Arms crossed in front of her, Shana glared at the couple as they walked into the main hall. It looked almost as if *she* was jealous of Lawrence and Darci, instead of the other way around.

"So what did you and Darci fight about before the gala?" Nancy asked Shana gently.

Leaning closer to Nancy, Shana glanced around to make sure no one was listening. "Everything," she said. "Darci accused me of trying to steal Lawrence away from her." Shana rolled her eyes. "Can you believe it? Why would I want to steal Mr. Steele?" She chuckled half-heartedly at her joke. "Then I told Darci that I was tired of all her sulking and little temper tantrums. I said I wasn't going to let her and Lawrence ruin the whole show for Madame."

"What did she say to that?" Nancy asked.

"Well, Darci claimed she didn't know what I was talking about, but I know she was lying. Then she kicked me out of her bedroom and said she wasn't going to go to any stupid party in my honor."

Nancy thought for a moment. It didn't sound as if Darci had planned the argument with Shana in advance, which meant she probably hadn't planned to skip the gala. But that didn't mean she and Lawrence hadn't schemed about breaking into the dance school. Maybe the argument had fit conveniently into their plans. That way, only Lawrence had been conspicuously absent from the gala.

But had Darci been the one who had rammed her and Bess with the van? Nancy frowned. It was hard to imagine that Shana's sister could have been that ruthless.

Suddenly, Nancy spied Madame alone by the buffet. "Come with me, Shana," Nancy said. "I want to tell Madame what happened tonight, and you should hear it, too."

The two girls wove their way through the groups of chatting parents. Nancy could hear a few people grumbling about all the problems that the school was having.

At the buffet table, Nancy got in line behind the directress and began to fill her plate with triangle sandwiches and stuffed mushrooms. "May I speak with you privately for a minute, Madame?" she asked in a low voice.

Madame looked up, a wary expression on her face. "Now, dear? In the middle of the party?"

Nancy nodded. "Yes. It's important that I talk with you before the police do."

At the word "police," Madame's eyes flew open and Shana gasped. Carrying their plates, the three of them found a quiet spot across the room.

Nancy told Shana and Madame about the Mouse King surprising them in the prop room and Lawrence showing up.

"What was Lawrence doing at the school?" Madame asked, sounding puzzled.

"He said he was just driving by," Nancy told her.

"It *is* sort of on the way to our house," Shana said.

Nancy nodded. "Yes, but Lawrence may have picked Darci up earlier and taken her to the school." Nancy then told Madame and Shana about the van ramming her and Bess in the Mustang. "Who has keys to the van?" she asked the directress.

"Why, Lawrence, of course." Madame thought a minute, then frowned. "In fact, besides me, he's the only one."

"Unless someone was able to copy the key," Nancy pointed out.

Shana shook her head. "I hate to say this, but it must have been Lawrence. It's so hard to believe he'd do something like that. . . ." Her voice trailed away.

"There must be some mistake," Madame scolded. "Lawrence has just been angry lately because he wanted to choreograph the whole show. I can't blame him, I suppose, but he'd never do anything to harm me or the school."

Nancy wasn't so sure about that, but she wasn't about to tell Madame. First, she needed some concrete proof.

"Thank you for telling me all of this, Nancy."
Madame patted her arm. "But I have to mingle
with all of the guests. This is my chance to
convince the parents that the school is just as
good as it always was."

Just then, a band in the front of the room
started to play. At the same time, Lawrence
strode through the crowd and up to Shana.
Sweeping one arm in front of him, he gave a low
bow.

"May I have this dance?" Lawrence asked with
exaggerated politeness. When he straightened
up, Nancy could see that he was trying to sup-
press a smile. "After all, I am your Cavalier."

Shana looked at him as if she wasn't sure if he
was serious or not. "It depends. Are you going to
waltz me into the dessert table? Or toss me over
your shoulder into the shrimp dip?"

Lawrence chuckled. "Only if you want me to,"
he teased. "It might give us good publicity for the
show."

Shana glanced over at Nancy.

"Sounds like an offer you can't refuse," Nancy
said lightly. She didn't blame Shana for hesitat-
ing, but she also didn't want to arouse Lawrence's
suspicions. Besides, something in Shana's expression made Nancy think that Shana really did want
to dance with Lawrence. Was there more going
on between the two of them than I'd thought?
Nancy wondered. Maybe they didn't dislike each
other so much after all.

"All right." Shana looked back at Lawrence.

"But the first time you step on my toes, I'm bowing out."

"It's a deal," Lawrence agreed. Shana put her hand on his arm, and the two of them headed toward the dance floor. Soon, Lawrence was gracefully twirling Shana around the other dancers in an old-fashioned minuet.

"Wow!" Nancy heard someone sigh beside her. Bess was staring at the couple with dreamy eyes. "Just look at those two dance. They're like the prince and princess in a fairy tale."

"Or the Sugar Plum Fairy and the Mouse King," Nancy commented ruefully. Bess gave her a puzzled look. But before Nancy could explain that she was pretty sure that Lawrence had had a hand in the thefts, she caught sight of Darci Edwards.

Shana's younger sister was standing with a group of girls her age. All their eyes were trained on Lawrence and Shana. The other girls' expressions were ones of admiration and delight, but Darci had a look of intense jealousy on her face. Her eyes were narrowed and her mouth was set in a grim line.

Suddenly, Darci turned and rushed from the room.

"I'm going to follow Darci," Nancy told Bess. "It's time I found out what's going on."

Nancy hurried from the dining room and into the main lobby. Darci Edwards was nowhere in sight. Then Nancy saw the door of the ladies room swing shut.

Striding across the oriental rug, Nancy headed down a short hall and pushed open the door. The lavish ladies room was empty, but Nancy heard a muffled sob coming from one of the stalls.

"Darci?" she called softly. "Are you all right? It's me, Nancy."

The sobs stopped abruptly. Someone blew her nose. "I'm fine."

Nancy shut the door behind her. "You don't sound fine."

"So? What do you care, anyway? You're Shana's friend."

"Yes. But I'm also a friend of Madame, and I'm interested in making sure *The Nutcracker* production goes smoothly."

There was a long pause. "So what does *that* mean?" Darci said in an angry voice.

"Why don't you tell me," Nancy challenged, folding her arms. She leaned back against the sink and waited.

Five minutes later, Darci opened the stall door and peered out. Her mascara had run beneath her eyes, giving her a haunted look. "Is anyone else here?" she asked warily. Nancy shook her head. With a sigh, Darci walked over to the sink. Grabbing a paper towel, she moistened it and dabbed at her eyes.

"Okay. So it's no secret that I hate Shana," Darci said bitterly. "And why shouldn't I? She took the part that should have been mine. Then she stole Lawrence."

Nancy raised one brow. *"Stole* Lawrence? I

97

didn't know you two were even dating. And from what I can see, Shana and Lawrence aren't exactly on good terms."

Darci snorted and threw the paper towel in the trash. "Yeah? Well, even hotshot detectives don't know everything."

Nancy wondered what Darci meant. But one thing was for sure: Darci was in no mood to confess. Nancy would have to try tripping her up. "You mean, things like who broke into the dance school?" Nancy said, studying Darci's face to see how the girl would react. But Darci just looked at her curiously, then opened her purse to pull out a lipstick. "Or who turned on the snow machine at rehearsal the other day?" Nancy continued.

Darci spun around. "That wasn't *me!*" she cried. Flinging her lipstick back into her purse, she pushed past Nancy and headed to the door. Her face was flushed, and she looked as if she was about to cry again.

"Darci, wait." Nancy grabbed the girl's elbow, but Darci jerked her arm from Nancy's grasp. "I'd like to help," Nancy said gently.

"No, you wouldn't," Darci spat out. "You just want to make sure that Miss Big Star Shana doesn't go back to New York. Well, I'm sorry Madame got hurt, but I wouldn't be sorry if my sister fell and broke her stupid neck!"

11

Terror in the Snow

Darci ran from the ladies room. Nancy sprinted after her, but when she reached the door, it swung toward her and she had to jump back. An elderly woman wearing a high-necked velvet dress and pearls had walked into the ladies room. It was Mrs. Farnsworth.

"Well, hello, Miss Drew," she said in a polite voice, but her gaze bore into Nancy like a drill. "Have you located my ornaments yet?"

Nancy was caught off guard. "Uh, no," she stammered. "But I know what happened to them," she added quickly, trying to edge around the woman. "In fact, that's what I've been working on tonight, so if you'll excuse me—" She flashed Mrs. Farnsworth a big smile, then squeezed past her and dashed into the lobby.

Seeing that Darci wasn't there, Nancy hurried

99

into the main dining hall. Shana was next to the dessert table, talking to Bess. Standing on tiptoe, Nancy scanned the crowd for Lawrence. Had he taken Darci home? Then she spotted him, next to Madame and several parents who appeared to be leaving with tired kids. Nancy checked her watch. It was almost eleven.

Bess caught sight of Nancy and waved. "Boy, you should have a piece of this cake," she said when Nancy walked up to her and Shana.

"Did you see Darci?" Nancy asked.

"Yes," Shana replied. "She burst in here a second ago and told my dad that she was feeling sick and wanted to go home. They're probably getting their coats."

"I guess Darci didn't confess," Bess said.

Shana shook her head. "There's no way Darci drove that van. My sister may have done some stupid things these last couple of days, and maybe she *was* trying to ruin the ballet. But she wouldn't hurt anyone on purpose."

Shana sighed heavily and set down her cake plate. "I'm exhausted. I guess I'd better round up my mother and Michelle. Dad will be back in a few minutes to get us. I'll see you two Monday, okay?"

Nancy and Bess nodded and waved goodbye. Then Nancy turned to the dessert table and cut herself a slice of cake. "I'm convinced I'm missing something," she told Bess, frowning. "I've been so sure the troublemakers were Lawrence and Darci that I haven't suspected anyone else. Maybe . . .''

"Oh, come on, Nancy," Bess chided as she studied a tray of cookies. "It has to be them. Shana's just sticking up for her sister. I mean, Lawrence and Darci are the only ones with motives, right?"

"True." Still, something was nagging at Nancy. Then she realized what it was that was bothering her: the footprints.

Plunking her plate on the table, Nancy twirled around. "Come on, we've got to go," she told Bess. "I need to check out those footprints before the snow covers them. We may be too late already."

"What?" With a look of dismay, Bess glanced at the dessert table, then back at Nancy. "We're going to leave all this?"

"Yup." Grabbing Bess's hand, Nancy began to lead her friend to the coatroom. "To make up for it, I'll owe you a sundae at Yogurt Heaven."

Soon Nancy and Bess were back in the dance school's parking lot. The snow had stopped, but now there was a confusion of footprints around the van.

"The police must have been here," Nancy guessed. "They were probably trying to verify that this was the vehicle that rammed us."

"How are you going to find Darci's prints in all this mess?" Bess asked.

Flicking on her flashlight, Nancy walked from

the van's passenger side to the road. "I'll have to find the path she made," she said.

Suddenly, Nancy bent down. "Here they are," she told Bess excitedly. "Just as I thought." Nancy shined the light on the perfect prints.

"Are you going to fill me in?" Bess asked. Her teeth were chattering, and she was rubbing her hands up and down on her coat sleeves. "Before I freeze to death?"

Nodding, Nancy stood up. "Those footprints are about the same size as Darci's, which is why I immediately thought she'd made them. But now I'm not so sure." She aimed the light closer. "Look at the pointy toes."

"So? Maybe Darci borrowed her mother's shoes."

Nancy flicked off the light. "Maybe. But if you were a teenager out to burglarize someplace, what would you wear?"

Bess thought for a moment. "Probably my flat-heeled boots or my tennis shoes."

"Exactly." Nancy started back to the Mustang.

Bess followed behind her. "Okay. So what do the pointy shoes prove?"

"Nothing," Nancy told her. "Yet. But maybe Shana's right. I need to stop concentrating on just Darci and Lawrence." When she reached the car, Nancy turned and gave Bess a troubled look. "There may be others who are out to ruin *The Nutcracker*."

* * *

"So what else did I miss?" George asked Bess and Nancy as they drove through the snow-covered pine forest. It was Sunday morning, and the girls were headed into the park to cross-country ski. "A car chase, a mouse-headed monster, and missing ornaments," George went on. "My ski party wasn't half as exciting."

Nancy laughed. "We're going with you today so we can forget all the excitement at the dance school."

"Boy, would I like to forget it." Bess yawned from the backseat of Nancy's Mustang. "I'm exhausted from all that sloshing around in the snow. Not that I would have picked skiing to help me forget. A buffet breakfast at some trendy new restaurant is more my style."

"That's for sure." George laughed. "I'm surprised you volunteered to go with us."

"It was either that or go into the dance school," Bess explained. "Madame actually called this morning to say that Mrs. Wolaski was showing up and would I like to come in and help. I had to think of a quick excuse. Going skiing with you two was the only thing I could think of."

"I talked to Madame this morning, too," Nancy said. "The police contacted her. The ballet school's van was definitely the one that ran into us. Fortunately, since Madame can prove she wasn't driving it, she won't be liable." Nancy frowned. "Unfortunately, Lawrence can't prove he *wasn't* driving it. The police said he has no alibi, except when he was with Darci, and that wasn't until later. And since Lawrence is an employee of the school, the school can be liable for the damages to all the other cars."

Bess groaned. "Oh, no. Poor Madame. She doesn't need lawsuits on top of everything else."

"Which means you've *got* to prove who was driving that van, Nancy," George said.

Nancy nodded as she pulled the Mustang into the parking lot. "And soon."

But half an hour later, when the girls skied into the park, Nancy tried to forget about Madame and her problems. The sun was sparkling through the branches of the pine trees, making the snow glisten. And since it was fairly early, the three of them had the trail all to themselves.

"Ready for something besides the beginner trail?" George called to Bess when they reached an intersection in the trails. She pointed up a hill with her ski pole.

"Uh, I don't know." Bess's cheeks were bright red from the cold and exercise. "I always forget how much work this is. Can't we go back and have lunch?"

With a grin, Nancy checked her watch. "It's only ten o'clock. And why would you want to be inside on such a great day?" She looked up through the trees. "Just look at that sky."

"Not without my dark glasses," Bess grumbled.

"Cheer up, Bess." George laughed at the disgruntled expression on her cousin's face. "It sounds like help is on the way. Hear that engine? Maybe it's a park ranger bringing us some hot chocolate."

Nancy looked up the intermediate trail. It sounded as if the snowmobile was coming down the steep hill.

Suddenly it zoomed into sight, bouncing over a ledge of rock and tearing down the trail toward them. Nancy caught a glimpse of the driver. He was wearing a black ski mask over his head.

"That's no park ranger," George called over her shoulder. "This guy's not supposed to be on the trail."

"Maybe we'd better tell him." Nancy slid her skis forward. The driver was going down the hill very fast, and instead of slowing down as he approached them, Nancy heard him accelerate. He was going to run right into them!

"Get off the trail," Nancy yelled, waving her ski pole at George and Bess.

Doing a neat turn, Nancy quickly coasted into the woods. Ahead of her, she could see George ski into a small grove of pines. But right behind her, Bess was still on the trail. Her left ski was crossed under her right one, and she couldn't move.

"Bess, hurry!" Nancy cried.

"I can't," Bess wailed. Suddenly, she toppled sideways, landing in the middle of the trail.

"Bess!" Nancy flipped her own skis around. But as she looked back up the trail, her heart caught in her throat. The snowmobile was barreling down, picking up speed. And the driver was leaning over the handlebars, steering right for Bess!

12

A Lost Clue

Nancy threw herself forward into the snow. Reaching in front of her, she grabbed Bess's ski jacket. Using all her strength, Nancy pulled her off the trail.

The snowmobile zoomed past in a spray of snow, running over the back tips of Bess's skis. Then it skidded to a stop, spun around, and faced them again.

"Look out! It's coming back!" Nancy screamed. Scrambling to her knees, Nancy tried to free her boots from the bindings.

"Nancy, get down!" she heard George yell. Looking up, she saw her friend standing in the middle of the trail. George's skis were off, and she was holding a tree branch in both hands like a baseball bat.

Dropping down, Nancy flattened herself against the snow. She could hear Bess breathing heavily beside her. But after seeing George, the snowmobiler apparently had second thoughts. With a roar of the motor, he turned around and headed away from them.

"Whew. That was a close one," George finally gasped. Throwing down the branch, she reached out her hand to Nancy. "Let me help you up."

Nancy struggled to her feet, managing to get her skis going in the right direction. "That was a close call," she said.

"Oooo. It feels like I broke both ankles," Bess said from the ground. Putting her hands under Bess's arms, George lifted her cousin up. Bess's skis angled wildly into the air, and her poles were on the other side of the trail.

Once she was safely on her feet, Bess gave George a pat on the back. "Thanks for scaring that creep off," she said. "Whoever it was, he sure wasn't fooling around."

"That's for sure," George agreed. As she walked over to get her own skis, George asked Nancy, "Who do you think it was? And why was he or she after us?"

Nancy shrugged. "I don't know. But I think we'd better get back and alert the park rangers. If it's some psycho, they'll want to know about it."

"And if he really was after us?" Bess asked.

"Then we should definitely be somewhere much safer," Nancy said in a grim voice.

"I bet that's the snowmobile the rental shop reported stolen," the park ranger said when the girls made their report. "Someone swiped it from a young couple who'd left it running while they got something out of their car. Sometimes it happens. Usually it's just kids out for a joyride."

"This wasn't someone joyriding," Nancy said. "The person was trying to run us down."

The ranger shook his head as he swung his legs from behind his desk. His office was in a big log building. In one corner of the building, a concession stand rented ski equipment. In another corner was a small cafe. Several couches were scattered around a roaring fire. Bess was sitting on the stone hearth, trying to get warm.

"I don't know what to tell you," the ranger said. "Usually, the only trouble snowmobiles cause is messed-up trails. We've never had someone report a snowmobiler going after them."

"Did the couple get a look at the person?" George asked.

The ranger shrugged. "Not a close one. They did say that he or she was not very tall and was wearing a ski mask and a green jacket."

Nancy and George exchanged glances. Lawrence was quite tall, so that ruled him out.

"We found it!" a deep voice said behind Nancy. A younger park ranger wearing a heavy parka strode into the office. "That snowmobile you described was abandoned at the edge of the park."

"Near a road?" Nancy asked.

The ranger nodded. "Either the thief had a car parked there or someone picked the person up."

109

"Oh, great," George grumbled. "Now we'll never know who did it."

Nancy stood up. "Well, thanks for all your help."

"And we're sorry you were inconvenienced," the older ranger said. After shaking hands with him, the girls joined Bess near the fire.

"Well?" Bess looked expectantly at her two friends.

Nancy let out a deep sigh. "The person got clean away. And we still don't even know if it was a man or a woman."

"Let's call the Edwardses' house and find out where Darci was this morning," George suggested. Digging through her coat pocket, she pulled out a quarter.

"Good idea." Nancy went over to a pay phone near the concession stand and dialed the Edwardses' number. Michelle answered on the second ring.

"Darci?" the young girl said, sounding surprised when Nancy asked for her sister. "Um, I think she's still asleep. My dad said we shouldn't bother her, since she felt so rotten last night."

"Could you call her, please?" Nancy asked. "Tell her Nancy Drew's on the phone."

Five minutes later, Michelle came back on the line. "She wouldn't open her door. She said to tell you to go jump in a lake."

"Mmmm." Nancy wasn't surprised. "Well, thanks anyway, Michelle."

When Nancy hung up, George and Bess looked at her expectantly. "Well?" they chorused.

"Darci said I should go jump in a lake," Nancy repeated.

"At least that proves she's home," George pointed out.

"Except Michelle said she wouldn't open the door. Maybe Darci had just sneaked back into the house."

"That's possible," Bess said. "The Edwards live in a ranch house, and Darci's bedroom is in the back. I remember from when I went to visit Shana years ago. Lawrence could've picked Darci up on the road and brought her home."

Nancy nodded. "That's one possibility. The other is that we're still on the track of the wrong person." Scooping up her gloves and hat, Nancy started out to the parking lot. "I think we need to change clothes and do some more snooping around at the dance academy. Maybe I've overlooked something important."

The dance school parking lot was deserted except for Madame's small foreign car and the school van.

"Oh, good," Bess said from the passenger seat. "Maybe Mrs. Wolaski went home. I'm just not in the mood for pinning and hemming."

"So what's our reason for being here?" George asked Nancy as they got out of the car. "What are we going to tell Madame?"

111

Nancy held up two small cans. "We'll tell her the truth. We're going to paint candy cane stripes on the pillars."

Bess groaned. "Suddenly, hemming sounds fun."

George and Nancy laughed as they went up the steps, through the front entrance, and into the hall. Madame's office door was shut. When they stopped in front of it, the girls could hear someone moving around the room.

"She must be working," Bess said, knocking lightly on the door. "There aren't any classes till two today, but she's probably here already. Madame?" she called. "It's Bess. Nancy, George, and I are going to be working in the prop room."

Bess knocked again, but there was no answer. The sounds had stopped. She gave Nancy a worried look. "Do you think everything's okay?"

Nancy turned the door knob. It was locked. "Madame?" she called loudly. "Are you all right?"

"Listen." George hushed them.

Nancy held her breath. Inside the office, she could hear a faint scraping sound. "Someone's opening the office window," Nancy whispered.

Spinning around, she dashed down the hall and pushed open one of the double doors in the back of the building. It swung open an inch, then clunked to a stop.

"What's the matter?" George asked.

Nancy peered through the inch-wide opening.

"The doors won't budge. Someone stuck a pole in the handles. Whoever was in Madame's office is getting away!"

"What's going on here?" a voice called from down the hallway. Madame Dugrand and Mrs. Wolaski were standing on the top of the basement steps.

"We heard someone in your office," Bess explained. "But the door was locked."

"And whoever it was jumped out the window, then barricaded the back door," Nancy added.

"What are you talking about?" Madame strode down the hallway, a key in her hand. "My door shouldn't be locked." Unable to keep up, Mrs. Wolaski hobbled a few steps behind the directress.

Inserting the key into the lock, Madame swung the door open and gasped. Drawers had been pulled out and dumped. Files and papers were scattered across the floor.

Stepping into the office, Nancy glanced at the front window. It was wide open. She dashed to the window and peered out. She could see footprints leading through the snow and around to the back of the building. "I'm going after our culprit," Nancy said. "Give me a boost, George."

Placing a hand under Nancy's knee, George lifted her friend onto the window sill. Nancy slid through, swung her legs around, and plopped into the snow. Then she raced to the back of the building.

113

But she was too late. The footprints led to car tracks, which turned off onto the dry road. Nancy had lost the culprit again.

Nancy clenched her fists in frustration. Then she bent down to inspect the footprints. They had the same pointy toes as the ones from last night.

Turning, Nancy retraced her steps, keeping her eyes trained on the ground in case the person had left another clue. Something glinted in the snow, catching her eye. Nancy immediately picked it up. It was a shard of glass.

She stuck it carefully in her coat pocket, then went up to the double doors in the back of the building. As she had guessed, a broom handle was stuck in the two door handles. The intruder had obviously been prepared, Nancy thought, so the break-in had definitely been planned. But by whom? And why?

When Nancy returned to Madame Dugrand's office, the directress, Bess, George, and Mrs. Wolaski were cleaning up.

"Is anything missing?" Nancy asked quickly.

Madame shook her head. "That's what's so strange," she said. "So far, nothing seems to have been taken. It appears that this is just another attempt to mess up the production."

"Wait a minute," Bess said. She was standing next to the desk, hanging up the framed photos that had been knocked to the floor. Stepping back, she surveyed the wall. "Didn't you have five pictures, Madame? Four on the outside and one in the middle? I've looked everywhere, but I can only find four."

"Hmmm." Madame moved around the desk to stand next to Bess. "You're right. But why would someone take a picture?"

Nancy pulled out the shard of glass from her pocket. "That's what this must be from," she said. "The glass covering the picture. Look, there are a few more pieces of glass on the floor below that wall," she added, pointing. "Whoever took the picture must have dropped it, and the glass broke."

"By why would someone take one of those old photos?" Mrs. Wolaski asked. The elderly wardrobe mistress had slumped into the office chair to rest her feet.

Nancy shook her head. "I don't know," she replied in a puzzled voice. "But the picture must have been stolen because it contained some kind of clue."

"What do you mean?" George asked.

Nancy looked up at the group in the office. Four pairs of eyes were staring expectantly at her.

"I'm not sure," Nancy said slowly. She swung her gaze to Madame. "But if you have another copy of that old photo, we may be able to solve our mystery!"

13

Shredded Dreams

Everyone turned to Madame Dugrand. "We're in luck," the directress replied. "I've saved all of my old photos, and I do have a duplicate of the picture that was stolen. It was from a *Nutcracker* production thirty-five years ago."

Stooping with the grace of an ex-dancer, Madame began sorting through a number of pictures scattered on the floor. Nancy knelt down beside her. "It looks as though our thief was hunting for the duplicate, too," Nancy said. "Who would know there was another copy?"

Madame shrugged. "Anyone, I suppose. I love to show off my photos."

"Here it is!" Bess announced from the other side of the desk. "It's the one of you in your Sugar Plum Fairy costume."

Madame stood up and took the picture from Bess. George and Nancy peered over her shoul-

116

der. The photo was of a group of dancers. A young Alicia Dugrand—in her late teens—was in the center, poised on her toes. The other dancers, all about the same age as Alicia, were dressed in their snowflake costumes and had their arms gracefully arched toward her.

"Who's that?" Nancy pointed to a ballerina on the far right. Instead of facing the photographer, she was glaring at Madame with a hateful expression.

"Oh, my." Madame sighed. "That's poor Grace Turner. A lovely dancer, but so competitive. She was furious that I got to dance the part of the Sugar Plum Fairy. She claimed I stole it from her, but I didn't. I had to work hard for that part."

Hmm, Nancy thought. Madame's tale sounded a lot like what was happening between Darci and Shana.

Mrs. Wolaski eased herself out of her chair. "I'm so glad you found that picture, Alicia," she said. "But if you'll excuse me, I must get back to my costumes."

"Of course, Gertrude," Madame replied. She seemed to be lost in thought.

"Could I see that picture again?" Nancy asked.

The directress nodded and handed the photograph to Nancy, who studied it closely. Since it was black and white, she couldn't even tell what hair color Grace Turner had.

"Whatever happened to Grace?" George asked.

Madame shrugged. "She eventually left the company, claiming the directors were against her. I don't know if she dropped out of ballet altogether, but I never heard her name mentioned again."

"Grace Turner," Nancy mused aloud. Something was trying to click in her mind. Then she remembered. "Grace Turner. G. T.!" Nancy said excitedly. Twirling around, she retrieved her purse from the top of the desk.

"G. T.?" Bess asked in a puzzled voice.

Nancy dug in her purse and pulled out the lace handkerchief. "They're the initials on the handkerchief I found on the stage after the fire."

Madame's head snapped up. "You're not suggesting that Grace Turner was involved in the fire? Why, that's crazy!"

"You've really flipped, Nancy," Bess said. "Grace would have to be . . . umm . . . over fifty years old now."

"Wait a second," George cut in. "Maybe it's not Grace, but someone who wants us to think it's Grace."

"Well, there's one way to find out." Nancy turned to Madame. "May I borrow this picture?" she asked.

"Why, certainly," the directress replied. "But please take good care of it. It's my last one."

Just then, Nancy heard a creak outside in the hallway. She glanced over at the door. It was halfway shut. Putting her finger to her lips, she signaled the others to be quiet, then tiptoed to the door. Carefully, she put her hand on the knob and flung it open. The hall was empty.

"Is anyone else here at the school besides Mrs. Wolaski?" Nancy asked Madame.

"Not that I know of," the directress said. "Shana should be arriving shortly to try on her costume."

Bess giggled. "Maybe it was the ghost of Grace Turner," she said.

"Right," Nancy muttered to herself. Maybe her ideas about Madame Dugrand's old rival had been a little farfetched, but at this point, Nancy wasn't going to rule out anything.

After helping Madame straighten the rest of the office, Bess, Nancy, and George went back out into the hall.

"What now?" Bess asked.

"We're off to the police station," Nancy replied, heading toward the front door.

"To report the theft?" George asked, puzzled.

Nancy chuckled. "I doubt the police would care that an old picture was taken. No, we're going to find out more about Grace Turner."

Half an hour later, Nancy, Bess, and George were in Chief McGinnis's office at the police station.

"I'll be glad to have our technician do an age progression on this," the chief said, holding the picture up. "We will have to blow the photo up first, though, so it'll be a bit grainy."

119

"What's an age progression?" Bess asked.

"Well, it's a process in which a computer scans a photo and is able to show what a person might look like however many years from now you want," Chief McGinnis explained. "It's a technique that's been used to track children who have been missing a long time."

"That's neat," George said. "So we'll be able to tell what Grace Turner looks like now."

The chief laughed. "Or what the computer thinks she should look like, anyway."

"That's what I need." Nancy had already given him a summary of what was going on at the school. "When will it be ready?"

"How about tomorrow afternoon?" The chief grinned at Nancy's impatient look. "I'm afraid the technician isn't even here on Sunday, so you'll have to hold your horses."

"Okay. We'll pick it up tomorrow." Nancy thanked the police officer, and the girls left the office.

"Where are we going now?" George asked.

Bess pulled a face. "Let me guess. Back to the dance school, right?"

Nancy grinned. "How'd you guess? I want to keep an eye on things. Besides, I have lots of work to do as prop mistress. But we'll stop off at Yogurt Heaven for lunch, my treat."

"Thanks." Bess sighed. "I'll need the energy. Knowing Mrs. Wolaski, she'll have plenty of sewing for me to do."

* * *

"So why do you think the snowmobiler tried to run us over?" George asked Nancy an hour later. The two girls were in the prop room, painting red and white stripes on the pillars. Nancy was standing on top of two boxes, trying to reach the top of a pillar.

"My guess is that the person was trying to scare us off." Nancy bent down and dipped her brush in the red paint. "Unless they really *were* trying to hurt one of us," she added grimly. "After all, with Bess or me out of the way, it would help foul up the production. There are only four more days until the dress rehearsal."

George looked up at Nancy and a drip of paint splattered on her cheek. "Hey!" George laughed. "Let's keep it on the pillars, okay?" Then her tone grew serious. "You know, until the snowmobile thing, nobody has really gotten hurt. But the snowmobile"—she shuddered—"could have broken both Bess's legs."

"Mmmm." Nancy stopped painting. "Well, if our culprits' plan is to sabotage *The Nutcracker*, then we've foiled them. So far, everybody's worked hard to keep the show on schedule. That means whoever the culprits are, they're starting to get desperate."

George nodded. "You're right. Now we just have to figure out who did it."

"Who did what?" a deep voice asked from the doorway.

Nancy swung around. Lawrence was leaning against the door frame, his hands clasped behind him. For a second, butterflies fluttered in Nancy's stomach as she wondered what he was holding. Another tire iron?

"We were trying to figure out who broke into the school," George answered.

Lawrence snorted. "That's easy. Ms. Drew and Ms. Marvin broke into the school. Then they made up a stupid story about some mouse attacking them."

Nancy jumped lightly off the boxes. "Oh, really?" she raised one brow. "Then who locked us in the prop room? You?"

Lawrence stepped forward, his arms still behind him. "You've already accused me once. Why don't you use your imagination? Maybe you girls locked yourselves in on purpose."

"Why, that's a clever thought." Nancy pretended to be surprised. She moved closer to George and out of Lawrence's reach. Even though he had a teasing smile on his face, she wasn't sure what he was up to. "And why would we do that?"

Lawrence shrugged. "To make me look bad. I think you're working with our prima ballerina, Ms. Shana Edwards. And I know she would do anything to keep me down."

Suddenly, the dancer thrust one hand from behind his back and into Nancy's face. Startled, Nancy jumped backward, knocking into George. Wide eyes and a wicked, toothy grin stared back at Nancy. It was the nutcracker doll.

Lawrence laughed. "Nasty-looking little fellow, isn't he? But he's as good as new. So how about putting him in a safe place until Thursday's dress rehearsal? I don't want to have to fix him again."

"You didn't need to scare us with him like that." George snatched the doll from Lawrence's hands.

Just then, a scream from the hall made all of them freeze.

"That's Shana!" Lawrence yelled, a horrified expression on his face. Turning, he dashed out the prop room door. Nancy and George raced down the hall behind him.

Nancy could see Shana standing at the top of the basement steps. The pretty dancer's green eyes were wide with horror as she cradled her Sugar Plum Fairy costume in her arms.

"Just look what someone has done to my costume!" Shana cried. "It's ruined." She held up the once-beautiful dress. Its satin bodice had been cut to shreds!

14

As Time Goes By

"Shana! Are you all right?" Lawrence asked, throwing his arms around the frightened dancer.

Tears welled in Shana's eyes. "Yes," she said shakily. "But when I went to the wardrobe room to try on my costume, I found it thrown into a corner." Shana held up the costume again. Jagged lines zigzagged through the satin bodice, and the wispy silver tulle skirt had been yanked from the top.

"It's been cut with very sharp scissors," Nancy said, fingering the ruined dress.

"What's going on?" Madame Dugrand came up behind Nancy. When she saw the costume, she let out a cry. "Shana! Your beautiful costume! Who would do such a thing?"

"Her costume?" a trembling voice broke in from down the hall. "Has something happened to it?"

Nancy turned to see Mrs. Wolaski come out of studio A, grasping Michelle Edwards's hand for balance. Michelle was dressed in her Clara nightgown. One sleeve had just been pinned on. Behind Michelle and the wardrobe mistress, Bess was carrying a tape measure and pin cushion.

Mrs. Wolaski's face paled as she hobbled toward Shana. Reaching out, she gently took the shredded garment from Shana's arms.

"All my hard work destroyed," she said in a quivery voice.

Madame put her arm around Mrs. Wolaski's shoulders. "Oh, Gertrude. I'm so sorry."

Michelle burst out crying and flung herself at her sister. "Shana. What are you going to do? Now you can't be the Sugar Plum Fairy, and—"

"Hey!" Bess broke in. She knelt down and put an arm around Michelle. "Have some faith. Mrs. Wolaski and I will perform a little magic and make your sister a whole new costume."

"Really?" Michelle sniffed.

"Really," Bess replied. But when Nancy glanced over at the white-haired wardrobe mistress, she wasn't sure the older woman was up to it. Her shoulders were slumped in defeat.

"This whole thing was directed at me," Mrs. Wolaski said, looking at Madame. "Everyone knows I spent weeks designing and making this costume."

"No. You're wrong," Shana said bitterly. "It's me the person's after." She looked directly at

Lawrence. "I think *you* did this to hurt me. You and Darci."

"Now wait just a minute," Lawrence retorted. "I'm sick of being Mr. Bad Guy. This show is just as important to me. Why would I ruin it?"

George spoke up. "Because you and Darci are both jealous of Shana."

"And you and Darci were the only two who weren't at the gala all night," Bess chimed in. "You had to be the ones who broke into the school and rammed our car."

Lawrence turned bright red. "That's crazy. You want to know what Darci and I did last night?"

"Yes," Shana replied in a quiet voice.

Everyone stared expectantly at Lawrence. For a second, he looked around at all the faces. Then he let out a sigh.

"All right. I didn't want to say anything, because Darci made me promise not to. She's afraid of what might happen, and . . ." He hesitated. "Well, she's kind of embarrassed."

"Excuse me," Mrs. Wolaski interrupted. "But I'd better go downstairs and work on Shana's costume. Maybe the skirt can be saved, and I can take a bodice from another costume, and . . ." Turning, she started down the steps, muttering to herself.

"I don't know why you're all so mad at Darci," Michelle said suddenly. "She's still at home. Dad's bringing her later. She couldn't have cut up the costume."

Shana sighed. "You just don't understand, Michelle."

"Maybe I should finish fitting Michelle's costume," Bess suggested. Taking the younger girl's hand, she led her back to studio A.

"So go on, Lawrence," Shana said, her voice trembling a bit.

He held up one hand. "Look, this isn't easy. I feel like I'm betraying Darci."

"Well, *someone* needs to explain what's going on," Nancy said. "The dress rehearsal is four days away. Whoever is trying to ruin the show is getting desperate."

Lawrence shook his head. "All I can do is tell you what happened and hope you'll believe me for once."

"I'll believe you, Lawrence," Madame said, patting his arm. "You've been like a son to me. I can't imagine you doing anything to hurt me."

"Thanks." Lawrence gave her an appreciative grin, then glanced at Shana.

Madame motioned them all to follow her down the hall. "I think we'd better discuss this in my office," she suggested.

When everyone had piled into the office, Lawrence took a deep breath. "Okay. I'll admit that, when Shana came back and Madame asked her to help with the choreography, I was plenty mad. I even tried to make Shana look bad at rehearsals, which I'm sorry for. It was stupid of me, and when Shana almost fell, well, I guess I realized how foolish I'd been."

He glanced up at Shana, his gaze apologetic. "I know now that you were only trying to help make *The Nutcracker* a success. You weren't trying to hurt me."

"What about Darci?" Nancy prompted.

"Well, Darci was really bent out of shape—big time," Lawrence continued. "She'd convinced herself that the part of the Sugar Plum Fairy would be hers. And"—his cheeks flushed—"she convinced herself that we had some kind of relationship. When I saw how overboard Darci was going, and how she was ruining the production for everyone, well, I tried to talk some sense into her."

Nancy nodded. "But she wouldn't listen."

"Oh, she listened," Lawrence said, running a hand through his blond hair. "She even admitted that she filled the snow machine with soap flakes and turned it on. She thought it would just mess things up. When she heard that Madame fell, she got pretty scared."

"And, uh, what about you and Darci?" Shana asked, stammering. Nancy saw a deep blush creep up the dancer's cheeks.

"Last night, before the gala, I told her we were just good friends," Lawrence explained, his eyes on Shana. "I guess Darci thought otherwise. She didn't take it real well."

Madame sighed and sat down on her office chair. "I feel this is all my fault. If only I'd noticed that everyone was so upset, I could have talked to Darci."

Nancy frowned and began pacing the short distance across the office. "No, it's not your fault, Madame. You had a lot on your mind. Someone made sure you had a lot on your mind. The fire, the ruined costumes, the stolen ornaments, Shana's near-accidents, the canceled programs." Halting in front of Lawrence, she gave him a stern look. "So what you're saying is, except for the snow machine, nothing else was Darci's fault."

Lawrence nodded. "That's the truth."

"Then we'll have to start working together to find out who's responsible for all of this." Nancy then told Shana, Madame, and Lawrence about the snowmobiler.

Lawrence whistled. "Wow. Someone means business."

"Actually, I think there are two people involved," Nancy said to Lawrence. "Which was another reason I suspected you and Darci."

Madame threw up her hands. "Maybe we should just cancel the whole production. Then no one will get hurt."

Nancy shook her head. "That's exactly what the culprits want."

"What's going on here?" a shrill voice cut in from the office door. All heads swung in that direction. Darci was standing in the doorway, looking from face to face with a stunned expression.

Then her gaze rested on Lawrence. "You told them, didn't you?" she accused. Tears started to spill down her cheeks. "Well, I hate you. I hate all of you!" She spun around, but Shana rushed over and grabbed her sister's arm.

"Darci, stop. There's been enough anger and jealousy. Lawrence had to tell us everything. We had to know that the two of you weren't involved in all the terrible things that have been happening here."

"But I *was* involved," Darci sobbed. "I didn't mean to hurt anyone. It's just that . . . I was so mad at everyone. And I thought no one cared about me."

"There, there." Madame pulled a tissue out of her pocket and advanced on the two sisters. "I don't blame you, Darci. If it had happened to me, I would have been upset, too."

Nancy remembered Madame's story about Grace Turner. If only they could get that age progression back this afternoon! She had a feeling the old photo held a very important clue.

Darci blew her nose loudly, and Shana put her arm around her sister's shoulders. "Feeling better?" Shana asked. Darci nodded.

"I know this is a little late," Madame said to Darci, a twinkle in her eye. "But since you know the dances already, how would you like to be the Sugar Plum Fairy in one of the matinees? That is, if it's all right with you, Shana," she added quickly.

Both girls nodded. Then Darci hugged Madame. "I'm sorry I caused so much trouble."

"No trouble, dear." Madame smoothed the younger sister's auburn hair.

Lawrence let out a deep breath. "Well, now that that's been resolved, what's the next step?" He looked at Nancy.

"Get back to work on *The Nutcracker*," Nancy answered. "Make sure it's the best production the dance school has ever put on. But," she warned, "don't forget—we're all in danger."

The next day, Monday, Nancy spent a lazy morning at home. She'd already called the dance school to make sure that nothing strange was going on. She passed the time by reading the newspaper and eating a leisurely breakfast.

But as the morning wore on, Nancy began to grow anxious. She was eager to get a look at the results of the age progression. Chief McGinnis laughed after she'd called him a second time.

"It'll be ready in an hour," he assured her. "The technician will leave it at the front desk."

Nancy phoned Bess and George, then ate a quick lunch. By the time she'd picked up her two friends and parked in front of the police station, exactly one hour had gone by. Once inside the station, the girls went straight to the desk.

"We're here to pick up a photograph," Nancy told the sergeant on duty.

"You must be Nancy Drew." He picked up an eight-by-ten-inch manila envelope and handed it to Nancy.

"Hurry and open it, Nancy," Bess urged.

Nancy pulled out two photographs and laid them side-by-side on the sergeant's desk. One was a blowup of Grace Turner from thirty-five years ago. The other was the computer's age progression.

Silently, the three girls studied the now older-looking woman. The computer had given her permed gray hair, thinner cheeks, and wrinkles under her eyes.

"What do you think?" George asked.

Nancy frowned. "The older Grace Turner looks quite a bit like the younger one. It doesn't remind me of anybody, but then, our culprit could be using a disguise now."

Then Nancy had an idea. Excitedly, she turned to the desk sergeant and asked him for a pencil.

"Let's try something," she said. Quickly, she began drawing on the photograph. She added glasses, wispy strands of hair, and bags under the eyes.

Bess leaned forward and peered down at the now enhanced photo. "Oh, no!" she gasped a second later. "It looks like Mrs. Wolaski."

"I'm afraid so, Bess," Nancy said. "There's a very good chance that Mrs. Wolaski is also Grace Turner—the only enemy Madame Dugrand has ever had!"

15

A Star in Peril

"Wait a minute." Bess frowned in confusion. "Mrs. Wolaski is really Grace Turner? That's crazy. Mrs. Wolaski is about seventy years old. And Grace Turner should be the same age as Madame Dugrand."

Nancy nodded. "Pretty clever disguise, huh?"

"So it's all an act," George said, nodding. "The limp, the cane, the hunched shoulders, how upset she was when Shana's costume was slashed."

Bess shook her head in bewilderment. "No way! Mrs. Wolaski slaved over that costume. She wouldn't have deliberately ruined it."

"Unless she thought it would take suspicion off her," Nancy explained. "Remember, she knew we'd found that photo. And I bet she was listening in the hall when I made the connection between Grace Turner and the initials on the handkerchief. She must have figured that someone would recognize her sooner or later."

"We'd better get back to the school and warn Madame Dugrand," George said.

Nancy nodded. "The faster the better."

When the girls reached the dance academy, they hurried straight to Madame's office.

The directress looked up when they knocked on the door. "Everything is falling into place now, thanks to you girls," she said with a smile. "The programs are here. Darci and Lawrence are rehearsing for the matinee, and Mrs. Wolaski managed to fix Shana's costume." Then she noticed the girls' crestfallen faces. "What's wrong?" she asked quickly.

"I'm afraid we have some bad news," Nancy told her. "Take a look at this." Bess pulled the two photos out of the manila envelope and laid them on the desk.

"I had your old photo age-progressed," Nancy explained. "There's Grace Turner thirty years ago . . . and here she is now."

"But this looks like . . . It couldn't be . . ." Madame Dugrand tilted her head to look up at Nancy. "Gertrude Wolaski?"

George, Bess, and Nancy all nodded. Her brow furrowed, Madame again studied the pictures. "So Grace really did come back to haunt me. After all this time. She really must have hated me that much." The directress sighed. "And I thought Gertrude volunteered to sew costumes because she loved ballet. How sad to think she was just waiting for a chance to get revenge."

"Where is she now?" Nancy asked.

"She's downstairs fitting Shana with her new costume," Madame Dugrand replied.

"Shana's alone with her?" Nancy asked, her voice rising.

"Why, yes. She went down about a half hour ago. Oh, I hope nothing's happened."

"Me, too," Nancy said in a grim voice. Quickly, she led the way out of Madame's office and down the hall to the basement door. But when the four of them reached the wardrobe room, they found it deserted.

"Oh, no!" Madame looked around the empty room. "What could have happened? I know they were down here half an hour ago."

Nancy squeezed the directress's hand. "Let's not panic yet," she said reassuringly. "Maybe they're in one of the studios."

Back upstairs, the girls and Madame spread out. First Nancy checked studio A. Lawrence and Darci were working on the pas de deux.

"Now what's wrong?" Lawrence muttered when Nancy waved him over. "It's bad enough that Roger, our so-called piano player, didn't show up."

But when Lawrence and Darci heard Shana was missing, they immediately volunteered to help. Pulling on their sweats and sneakers, they followed Nancy into the hall. As they rushed

135

down to the next studio, Nancy explained about the photo and why they were looking for Mrs. Wolaski.

Ten minutes later, everyone had gathered in Madame's office. The entire building had been searched, but there was no sign of Shana or Mrs. Wolaski.

"Did Shana drive today?" Nancy asked.

Madame nodded. "But I picked up Gertrude at her house."

"Then that's where we'll look next." After Madame gave her Mrs. Wolaski's address, Nancy quickly put on her coat and headed outside. Lawrence, George, and Bess followed. Darci and Madame stayed behind to call the Edwardses' house, just to make sure Shana hadn't been picked up by someone.

But when Nancy checked the parking lot, Shana's beat-up Ford was in its usual place beside Madame Dugrand's small foreign car.

"Nancy, take a look at this!" George called from the corner of the building. Nancy, Bess, and Lawrence ran toward her through the snow. George held up a gold bracelet that glistened in the sun.

"It's Shana's!" Lawrence exclaimed. "She *never* takes it off. Not even for rehearsal. She must have dropped it on purpose."

"Stay here a minute," Nancy told the others as she hurried around the side of the building. She didn't want anyone accidentally messing up the footprints.

136

Nancy slowly walked forward following the same path the thief had taken the day the photo had been stolen. Studying the tracks, she found her own footprints from Sunday, then the pointy-toed prints. Mixed in with the two was a third pair of prints, which moved straight ahead. Besides them, a smaller set of prints seemed to zigzag back and forth.

Nancy bent down to take a closer look. At one point, the third set of footprints turned into slide marks in the snow, as if someone had been dragged.

Nancy's heart quickened. If Shana had dropped the bracelet, then one of these sets of prints was hers. And if Nancy's hunch was right, they were the ones that zigzagged. That probably meant that Shana wasn't traveling under her own free will.

Following the tracks, Nancy reached the road behind the dance school. There, she found new tire marks on the side where someone had pulled over. Then she saw the pointy-toed prints mingling with the other two. Obviously, Gertrude Wolaski had a partner. But who?

Nancy tried to imagine what happened. Mrs. Wolaski had gotten Shana out to the parking lot on some pretense. Then, once outside, she'd somehow forced the dancer behind the building, where Mrs. Wolaski's accomplice had been waiting. Nancy took a deep breath. In other words, Shana had been kidnapped.

"It's time to call your friend Chief McGinnis,"

Lawrence said, after Nancy had returned to the others and told them what she'd found.

"I know just what he'll say," Nancy replied. She deepened her voice. " 'Until someone's been gone for forty-eight hours, or unless we discover a ransom note, there's nothing we can do.' " Nancy sighed. "Actually, we don't even have definite proof that Shana was kidnapped. It's just my gut feeling."

"And your gut feelings are usually right," George added.

"So what are we going to do?" Bess asked anxiously.

Nancy headed for the school's front door. "First, we tell Madame. Then we pay a visit to Gertrude Wolaski's house."

"But why would Gertrude kidnap Shana?" Madame Dugrand asked when she'd gotten over the initial shock. Darci had gone back to studio A to gather the rest of her things.

"What better way to hurt you, Madame, than to kidnap the star of your show?" Nancy replied.

The directress put her head in her hands. "This is all so terrible," she said in a shaky voice.

"We're heading to Gertrude's house right now," Nancy told her.

"I'm coming with you," Madame insisted, slipping on her coat. "We'll take the van. It will hold all of us easily."

"Maybe you should stay here, Bess," Nancy suggested. "We'll check back as soon as we find out something. If you don't hear from us in an

hour, call Chief McGinnis and tell him everything."

Bess's face fell. "But what if Mrs. Wolaski
comes back here, and I'm all alone?"

"I doubt she'll show her face here ever again,"
Nancy reassured her friend. "Get Darci to stay
with you. She'll want to keep her parents posted,
too."

"Okay." Bess tried to grin bravely.

A few minutes later, as Madame drove down
Galworthy Road, the sky began to darken. Nancy
pointed to a gray clapboard house with a front
porch. "There it is. Pull up on the other side,
Madame."

"Unless they're sitting in there in the dark, no
one's home," George commented as Madame
parked across the street. "What do we do now?"

Nancy pulled her collar up over her neck. "I
guess we knock first, and if no one answers—"

"We bust the door down," Lawrence growled
as he threw open the van door. "Whoever kidnapped Shana is going to pay."

"Well, that's not exactly what I had in mind,"
Nancy said as she followed him out of the van.
Her heart was pounding as the four of them
approached the house. The street lights hadn't
clicked on yet, so everything seemed dark and
shadowy. Quietly, Nancy walked up the porch
steps, tightly gripping her flashlight. To make
sure they weren't caught in the act, they wouldn't
turn the lights on once they were inside.

When she reached the front door, Lawrence

stepped next to her. He held a tire iron in his hand. "I brought it just in case," he said in a low voice.

Nancy nodded. "We may need it," she told him. "Gertrude's accomplice, whoever he is, is probably here, too." Then she leaned forward and rang the bell. There was no answer.

George walked over to one of the windows and peeked in. "The curtains are drawn tight. I can't see a thing."

"We're going in," Nancy said grimly. She tried the knob, then opened her shoulder bag and took out her lock-picking kit. A few moments later, the door swung open.

As soon as Nancy stepped inside, it was obvious that this wasn't just the home of Gertrude Wolaski. It was also a shrine to the former ballerina Grace Turner. Nancy shined her flashlight on the hallway walls, which were papered with photos and newspaper articles. Pictures of Grace in different costumes were placed all around the living room. Ballet memorabilia were strewn on every table and shelf, and a pair of faded pink toe shoes hung over the mantel.

"How sad," Madame Dugrand murmured as she looked around her. "I wish Gertrude had told me who she was. Grace Turner was her stage name. I never knew her as Gertrude. Maybe I could have helped her work out her anger."

"I don't think so," Nancy said, pointing to a picture on the living room wall. It was the stolen photo of Alicia Dugrand in her Sugar Plum Fairy costume. The glass over the photo was broken, and a large red X was marked across the young dancer's face.

Madame Dugrand shook her head sadly. "Poor Grace," she said.

"Hey, look at this," Lawrence called from the other side of the room. He had opened a large wooden box he'd found in a corner. "Mrs. Farnsworth's antique ornaments."

George and Nancy rushed over. When Nancy saw that the valuable decorations—made of delicate glass in all shapes and colors—were in perfect condition, she gave a sigh of relief. "Now, if we can just find Shana. Let's split into pairs and search the house. Look for anything that might give us a clue to Mrs. Wolaski's accomplice or another address."

Lawrence and George nodded, then headed for the kitchen. Nancy and Madame crept silently up the steps. Two rooms and a bath opened into the narrow hall. Nancy peered into the first room. It was Gertrude's bedroom. Drawers were flung open and clothes were strewn on the bed, as if someone had been in a hurry. Something fuzzy was sticking out from under the bed. When Madame caught sight of it, she grabbed Nancy's arm, startled.

Nancy bent down to pick up the fuzzy object. It was Mrs. Wolaski's wispy-haired wig. "I guess she doesn't need this anymore," Nancy said grimly. She motioned for Madame to follow her. "Let's check the other room."

It was a small, sparsely furnished office. Nancy walked over and opened the front of an oak desk, shining the flashlight beam on a stack of envelopes. "Here's a bank envelope with canceled checks," she said. "Maybe they'll tell us something. Why don't you look through them?" she added, handing the envelope to Madame. Then Nancy began to examine the other envelopes. Letters, bills . . .

A tap on her arm made Nancy look over at Madame. The directress was staring at a handful of checks. "Nancy, look at these."

Nancy shined the flashlight on the canceled checks. Then she took them from Madame and looked closely at each one. There were ten checks in the amount of five hundred dollars, and every one of them was made out to Roger L. Wolaski.

They'd found Gertrude Wolaski's accomplice!

16

Pas de Deux

"Roger L. Wolaski," Nancy murmured. "Do you think the *L* could stand for Lutz?" she asked Madame.

"Lutz must be his middle name," Madame replied. Then she gasped. "You mean Roger is Gertrude's *son?*"

"He may be her son or some other kind of relative," Nancy said. "It makes sense, I guess. It would be hard to recruit a total stranger to help carry out a loony plan like Gertrude's."

When Nancy and Madame made their way back to the living room, Lawrence and George reported that the rest of the house was deserted. Nancy explained Roger's role in the scheme, and that he was somehow related to Gertrude.

"Roger Lutz is working with Mrs. Wolaski?" Lawrence said after Nancy had told him and

George the news. "But he's such a mousy little guy."

"Roger has to be Gertrude's accomplice," Nancy replied. "He had access to the building. And since he was always way in the background, no one suspected him." She showed Lawrence and George the canceled checks.

"I never suspected they were related," George commented. "Mrs. Wolaski acted as if she didn't even know Roger."

With a dejected expression, Madame slumped down on the sofa. "How could I have been so blind? I even saw Roger sneaking around on the day of the fire and never paid any attention. Those two were sabotaging my school right under my nose."

"Now we have to figure out where they took Shana," Nancy said. "Madame, when you hired Roger, did you get an address?"

"Oh, my, I didn't!" Madame's shoulders slumped even more. "I was just so glad to have someone play the piano for free. He seemed like such a nice man."

Nancy began pacing back and forth. "Okay, everybody think. Did Roger ever mention where he lived? Or mention anything at all about where he lived? Like he lived with his parents, or in an apartment? And how about a license plate number, or even what his car looked like?" Nancy stopped and looked at the others, but their expressions were blank. "How about what college he went to?" she tried again.

Lawrence shook his head. "The guy never said 'boo' to anyone."

"I'll call Bess and Darci to tell them what we found out." George started toward the kitchen. "Maybe one of them knows something."

While she waited for George to return, Nancy continued to pace, trying to figure out what to do next. They could call the police. But what would they tell them? That the four of them had broken into a house? That would go over well with the River Heights police.

Suddenly, George rushed back into the room. "I think I've got a clue!" she said excitedly. "Darci remembers Roger talking about his brand-new apartment."

Lawrence snorted. "Well, that narrows it down to about a hundred or so, just in River Heights."

Brand-new apartment, Nancy thought, and then something clicked in her mind. "That's it!" she cried. "Come on, everyone. I know where Roger lives!"

When they were back in the van, Nancy gave directions to Madame and explained how she'd figured out that Roger lived in the new garden complex for singles. "That's where the van was heading on the night Bess and I followed it. Roger must have been taking my ornaments back to his apartment. When he spotted us, he turned the tables and started to chase us."

"But how are we going to figure out which is his apartment?" Lawrence asked doubtfully. He was in the passenger seat, holding tight to the door. Madame was driving as quickly as she could without breaking any laws.

Nancy told her to take a sharp right, and they turned into the main street of the complex. As the van slowed, she studied all the entrances carefully. "If I'm remembering correctly, the van pulled out of this drive and began to tail us." She pointed to the second entrance on the left.

Just then, Madame hit the steering wheel with the palm of her hand. "A blue foreign thing!" she declared.

"Huh?" Lawrence swung around. "You mean, that's what Roger drove?"

Madame nodded emphatically.

"All right!" From the backseat, George gave the directress a pat on the shoulder.

Madame turned the car into the complex and began to cruise alongside the line of parked vehicles. The road curved in a semicircle in front of the four apartment buildings. Nancy counted four small blue cars.

"Now what?" George asked in a gloomy voice. "We can't knock on every door."

"Pointy-toed shoes," Nancy reminded her friend as she swung the car into a parking spot.

"Would you mind speaking English?" Lawrence said.

Nancy opened the van door. "We need to look for pointy-toed footprints in the snow. Roger must have been the one wearing shoes like that."

Excitedly, the four of them got out and began

146

to look around. When Nancy searched the snow on the curb by the last blue car, she found what she was looking for: footprints with clearly pointed toes. They led directly to the third building. Quietly, the four of them stepped into the outside foyer.

They all stood in front of the rows of mailboxes, and Nancy said, "Look." She pointed to the white strip under the box for apartment 3B. R. L. Wolaski was written on it.

"So do we call the police now?" George asked.

Lawrence held up his tire iron. "No way. It's four against two. By the time the police come blasting in here, who knows what Grace and her whacky sidekick will have done to Shana."

Nancy turned and laid her hand on Madame's arm. "Madame, why don't you take the van and drive to the nearest phone? Call Chief McGinnis and tell him to send a squad car over."

"No," Madame replied firmly. "I want to confront Grace myself."

"I'll do it, Nancy," George offered. "I'll call Bess and Darci, too." Grabbing Madame's keys, George hurried back to the car.

Nancy took a deep breath. "Now it's only three against two."

"Yeah. But we do have the element of surprise," Lawrence said.

"Maybe. Unless they've been watching us from a window." Motioning the others to stay put, Nancy walked back to the sidewalk and looked up. The two windows on the third floor were dark. Were Mrs. Wolaski and Roger just pretending not to be home?

Nancy rejoined Lawrence and Madame Dugrand in the foyer.

"I'm ready." Madame's eyes were determined.

Nancy took a deep breath. "Then let's go."

Cautiously, the three of them went up to the third floor. Nancy put her ear to the door of apartment 3B and listened. All seemed quiet.

She took her lock-picking kit from her purse and unlocked the mechanism.

When she quietly swung the door in, she saw the apartment was dark. When her eyes adjusted, Nancy was surprised to see Shana sitting in a chair in the center of the room. Her mouth was gagged and her hands were tied behind her with rope. Shana looked at Nancy with frightened eyes. Then she tried to cry out in a muffled voice.

"Shana!" Lawrence shouted, pushing past Nancy.

"No! It's a trap!" Nancy cried. Grabbing Lawrence's arm, she tried to stop him. But it was too late. Someone sprang from behind the door and whacked Lawrence on the back of the head with a cane. The dancer crumpled to the floor.

It was Roger. He turned and smiled wickedly. "Welcome, Ms. Drew." He raised the cane menacingly.

Just then, out of the corner of her eye, Nancy glimpsed something that would help her out of her predicament. It was the Mouse King headpiece, which she figured Roger and Mrs. Wolaski had stolen in a last-minute attempt to ensure that the ballet would be ruined.

Without giving Roger a moment to react, Nancy picked up the headpiece and swiftly yanked it over his head.

From inside the Mouse King head Roger emitted a muffled squeal of anger as he groped for Nancy. She had put the piece on backward, so that Roger was completely blinded and had no idea where he was standing in relation to Nancy. He turned in a semicircle, desperately swinging the cane to try to strike her.

Nancy tried to grab the cane, but just then Roger stumbled on a coffee table and, with a screech, fell to the floor. Crouching down, Nancy dug her fingernails into Roger's skin, squeezing the tendon in his wrist, hard. He immediately cried out in pain and loosened his grip on Gertrude's cane.

Nancy tossed the cane to the other side of the room, then looked around for something with which to tie Roger. She grabbed the gold tie cord from the drapes behind her and quickly bound his wrists together. Madame came running up with the tie cord from the other set of drapes, and Nancy expertly wrapped and knotted it around Roger's ankles. Finally, she pushed the sputtering man into an arm chair. "Don't move," she told him.

Roger whined something unintelligible from inside the costume. Just then, a commotion in the hall made Nancy turn and step out. Madame Dugrand was grappling with someone at the top of the steps. Nancy had been so busy subduing Roger that she hadn't heard Mrs. Wolaski approaching. The ex-wardrobe mistress was attacking her prime target—Alicia Dugrand.

"Madame!" Nancy cried out. Gertrude had the directress bent over the stair railing. Madame's eyes were wide with horror.

Dashing forward, Nancy grabbed Gertrude's arm and tried to pull her off. To Nancy's surprise, Madame suddenly gritted her teeth and gave a powerful shove, throwing Gertrude against the wall.

Without her makeup and wig, Gertrude Wolaski looked very different. She had short brown hair, very few wrinkles, and a trim build.

"You're not winning this time!" Gertrude shouted to Madame. Hands raised like claws, she rushed for Madame's face. The directress nimbly jumped sideways. Then, reaching out with her leg, she kicked Gertrude in the thigh. Gertrude stumbled sideways and lost her balance. Then, with a cry, she rolled down the steps.

Madame stared down the steps in silent horror. Her attacker was sprawled on the second floor landing, not moving. "Oh, Nancy. I didn't want to hurt her." Madame clutched Nancy's arm.

"She gave you no choice," Nancy told her gently.

Just then, two police officers came running up the stairs. They stopped on the second floor landing and looked down at the body, then up at Nancy and Madame Dugrand.

Behind the two officers was Chief McGinnis. His gray brows shot up in surprise. "Nancy, are you all right? Your friend called and explained what was going on, but I had no idea."

Nancy nodded. "There's another one up here." She pointed to the open apartment door. Roger sat in the chair grunting angrily as he tried to free his wrists. The headpiece had twisted to the side, so that it looked as though the Mouse King was looking right at Nancy.

She stepped inside the room to find Shana sobbing in Lawrence's arms. He had untied her and was stroking her hair. Now that Nancy could see that everyone was okay, she wearily slumped against the wall. It was finally over.

"From what Roger has confessed," Chief McGinnis told Nancy, George, and Bess on Friday night, "it was all Gertrude Wolaski's idea. She contacted Roger—who is her nephew—about six months ago, and even set him up in the apartment."

"And he needed money, so he went along with everything," Nancy guessed.

The chief nodded. "Roger claims his aunt assured him that no one would get hurt, which is the only reason he decided to help her. But I don't know, these two both seem a little nuts to me."

The four of them were standing outside the

dance academy's recital hall. Chief McGinnis was wearing a suit and tie, and Nancy, George, and Bess had on holiday dresses. Inside the hall, a large crowd was waiting eagerly. It was opening night of *The Nutcracker*.

"And what about Gertrude?" Bess asked. "She was lucky she only broke her leg in the fall."

The chief shook his head. "Gertrude claims that there is no such person as Grace Turner. She says Madame Dugrand made that whole story up."

"What? That's crazy," George interjected. "We saw Gertrude's house. It was wall to wall with Grace Turner's ballet pictures."

"Poor Gertrude," Nancy murmured. "She's still trying to get at Madame."

The chief nodded. "Right. But with Roger telling us everything, she won't get too far. He's admitted to stealing both sets of ornaments, starting the fire, and loosening the barre. He claims his aunt did everything else."

"What about ramming us with the van?" Bess asked, her hands on her hips. "And almost running me over with the snowmobile?"

"Well, he's hedging on those, since they're pretty stiff charges. But I think we'll nail him."

Nancy sighed. "I'm just glad we caught those two in plenty of time. We all worked really hard, and I think this year's *Nutcracker* is going to be fantastic."

Chief McGinnis's eyes twinkled. "And I'm sure Madame will be happy to hear that I talked

152

to my old friend at the firehouse. He's agreed to extend the time she has to fix those violations."

Bess peered into the recital hall. "If the next three nights are this crowded, it should help straighten out the school's financial problems."

"And with all the good publicity, Madame should get some of her students back." Nancy nodded toward the front of the hall. Several reporters were sitting in the front row.

"I almost fainted when Lawrence and Shana danced the pas de deux yesterday at the dress rehearsal," Bess said dreamily. "It was *too* romantic."

Nancy smiled. "I guess they finally realized how much they care about each other."

"Well, I'm glad everything turned out so well," Bess said. "Lawrence is even going back to New York with Shana. Can you believe it? He's determined to make it this time."

"And Darci will be the top dancer at the school," Nancy added. "That should make her happy."

Just then, the lights began to dim.

"I think we'd better get to our seats," Chief McGinnis said. The four of them hurried down the aisle, sitting down just as the curtain began to rise, revealing the Christmas party scene of the first act.

When Nancy saw how beautiful the stage looked, even she had to gasp. Mrs. Farnsworth's ornaments glittered and danced in the spotlight that shone on the Christmas tree. The graceful dancers began to twirl onstage in their gorgeous costumes, all bearing gifts, including the nutcracker doll for young Clara.

George leaned toward Nancy. "Another successful *Nutcracker* performance," she whispered. "Thanks to Nancy Drew!"